MW01224254

# Through the Gates: The Blood Princess Saga Books 1-3

Revised Editions Copyright 2015-2016 Jessica Short
Cover Illustration by Anson
Published by Jessica Short at Smashwords

# Best Laid Plans: The Blood Princess Saga Book 1

# Acknowledgements

It has been said so often that it has almost become a cliché, but it really is true: nothing is created in a vacuum. So it is with this novella, it would not have been created if not for the following people.

To Matt G: for being so laid back and nonjudgmental that a scared writer could show him a half-finished kink story and *know* that his opinion of said writer would not change.

To Matt O: for taking enough of an interest in the story to argue with the writer how best to handle issues. While I didn't take every suggestion I took enough to dramatically improve the story.

To Anson: for allowing me to use the image he created as my cover. If you like his work then I'd suggest taking a look at his other pieces at http://anson7.deviantart.com.

And a special thank you to a new friend: J.B.H. a professional editor who put up with an author who had never worked with one before. His help has only improved this work.

Finally, and a no less important a thank you to Gary Gygax; for creating a game that made me want to read and then want to tell stories.

# Chapter One

'You have no idea how the world really works.' How many times have you heard that from someone? It could be a mid-level house functionary, a bartender, or a beggar on the street, hells *I've* even said it a few times. When most people say it, they're talking out of their ass (I include myself in that group by the way) so when you actually run into a situation that proves just how little you actually know about the world, it can really slap you around. For me this slap coincided with the job that got us noticed by the upper level of the Compact.

Said job started this morning, when the Asters sent the word out that they needed the Blood Princess and her Black Bitches for a rush mission. Three days ago, the head of House Aster's teenage twin daughters had been kidnapped. The most likely culprit was the most powerful house of the Compact -the group of families and individuals who ran the city- House Hector. House Hector was responsible for diplomatic efforts into the elemental realms. Their influence drove like tendrils deep into these planes of existence. As deep, if the rumours were correct, as the Demon Pits themselves. These diplomatic efforts resulted in pacts and treaties that allowed the Compact to generate much of its wealth from the inter-dimensional gates from which the city took its name.

Aster had tried to confront the Hectors head on, but had lacked the political capital to do so successfully. In fact, Shon Aster had to pay fines for slandering the Hectors when he had accused them in public without enough proof (or enough coin) to convince the other Compact families of his claim.

While the Asters might have lacked the influence within the Compact, they did have enough gold to 'influence' others. This is where I entered the story.

So I guess it's a good time to introduce myself: my name is Annabell, Annie for short, and I'm professionally known as the Blood Princess. I'm Human, and have seen 18 summers. I'm tall for a city girl standing 5'6". Thanks to my constant physical training, I have the type of athletic body that draws lustful glances or jealous looks, depending upon your preference. Thanks to a night of partying with one of my partners I now have blood red hair and loud permanent makeup (Never tell an exhibitionist nymphomaniac that you want to do something wild. Trust me on this one).

I'm a mercenary, specializing in 'thorny problems'. A fighter by training, I have a preference for heavy kopis knives as my main weapons. Granted they're not as deadly as broadswords or two handed axes, but in the close confines of a city alleyway or crypt where I do most of my fighting, they're far more effective.

It's also the reason for my professional name; knife fighting is always up close, and the blood tends to get everywhere.

But enough about me, the twins still needed to be rescued. It took a bit of Aster's gold in the right palms for us to find out that the Hectors did indeed have the twins. But knowing and proving something are two very different things. We also discovered that they were going to be shipped out of the city early tomorrow morning. Since this is The City of Gates, 'shipped out' means that they were going to be sent to another plane of existence. My team and I therefore were a bit rushed to do something.

The plan that we decided to go with was created by Susa, our resident smart person (and the aforementioned nymphomaniac exhibitionist). It entailed her and I getting caught sneaking in to where the twins were being held. Lia, another team member, would be sneaking in separately to us. Her role was to find us, and then help us escape with the twins. Our last and least known member of the team, Gwen, would be waiting for us outside with horse and cart to get us all out of the neighbourhood.

I know, not the sanest of plans, but just wait on passing final judgement. Lia is the best cat burglar in the city; she could have gotten in and out of the Hector compound herself, but there is no way she could have gotten out with the twins. And while Susa and I aren't ogres when it comes to stealth, we couldn't follow the paths that Lia took. Susa's plan, while crazy, got all of us in and gave us a chance of getting out with the twins. Of course there were holes in the plan a dragon could fly through, but I've always been good at thinking on my feet.

The plan however did beg one big question. What to wear to your own capture? Obviously you don't wear your best, but at the same time, you don't want to give away that you're not bringing your A game.

First thing you do is apply a mixture of ash and fat over your body. Since some places are difficult to get to it's best to do this with someone. So Susa and I did each other. As we did so, I couldn't help but glance over at Susa's naked body.

In The City of Gates the female form is seen as the pinnacle of perfection. Women are meant to worship at this pinnacle as much as men to the point where the expectation is that a woman will have both male and female lovers. This is one of the city's social norms I readily agree with.

The city is extremely hot and humid during the day, cooling down to hot and humid at night. This along with the high elves having a lock on the definition of beauty, pretty much dictates fashion. So like most Human females our age both Susa and I had gone "Elven", having paid for minor magic to permanently remove all body hair. Both mundane and magical body art and body modification of all kinds has been in vogue for the past 50 years; for example, Lia, Susa and I all sport nipple, navel, and clit rings along with a matching stud through our tongues. Not to mention at least three tattoos apiece. In my case, I have a half sleeves on each arm and one on my lower back. (Long story which involved the 'let's do something wild' night)

However the modifications that Susa has are extreme even for this city. She's just over 5' tall and maybe weighs 90 lbs wet, yet she has perky breasts that look large on her petite frame; her skin is a deathly pale white which never tans nor burns under the sun, and her shoulder length hair is a flat black that almost absorbs light. Her eyes are coal black as are her lips, fingernails and toenails. However her vulva lips and nipples are also black in colour, which offsets the silver rings she wears through them. This is not the end of her body modification: arcane tattoos circle her upper arms, thighs, groin, and lower back. Finally (when it's not leering at me), Susa's familiar, a foot tall imp named Ordis, rests on her right shoulder blade as a final piece of body art. She claims that all of these modifications were the result of her coven, buts she's wild at the best of times, so sometimes I have my doubts.

As we were getting to our armour, Susa said "You are aware there is a pretty good chance when we get caught they're going to strip and torture us right? And this isn't going to be like your sessions with Brutal; there's no safe words, and they'll have absolutely no qualms about leaving marks."

I had been aware of that possibility, and while the idea was scary I also felt strangely excited: I have a preference for rough sex and I've been in a yearlong relationship with one of the city's best dominants. Brutal (yes that really is his name) is not exactly a lover for me as much as a personal trainer. I've pushed both my pain and endurance tolerances further with him than all the drill instructors or weapons masters in the past combined.

But I also knew that this wasn't a place for idle fantasy. "Yes, I'm aware of that," I replied. "But it's a chance we'll have to take. Besides, if we're lucky, we won't be there long enough for them to get too creative."

Then smiling coyly I reached over and ripped Susa's G string off her hips. Before she could react, I took the G string that I was going to wear and threw both into the fire. "Since we're going to be stripped there's no reason to wear those, then, is there?" I asked.

Susa just looked at me for a second. "True," she said finally, then continued to get dressed.

For armour, I decided upon a black sleeveless studded leather body thong. This gave me suitable body protection but still the freedom of movement and endurance I prefer in combat. As I've said, The City of Gates is hot and humid all year round. So despite leaving my arms and legs bare the body thong actually passed as heavy armour in the city.

Over the armour, I strapped on a wide leather belt that rode low on my hips to carry things like a silk rope, lock picks, and a couple of healing potions. I then strapped on a pair of metal epaulettes thick enough to stop all but the hardest of blows, so that my shoulders and neck were protected.

A pair of blackened steel bracers protected my lower arms. Normally these are enchanted devices that strengthen my blows, but tonight they're just a normal set. Over my hands I had on a pair of blood red spiked fighting gloves. On more than one occasion I have found that a surprise jab to the nose with a fist has been an effective way to beat a defence when other means have failed. My lower legs were protected by a pair of knee high red leather boots which again offered a reasonable balance between protection and flexibility of movement. On my head I wore a broad metal head band wrapped in black leather to make it more of a target over my red hair.

For weapons I took my two practice kopis. Their heavy concave designs creates a cutting force that is comparable to longer blades or axes, but in a much smaller weapon. These I strapped onto my fighting belt and tied the sheaths down to my upper legs. While not the same quality as my normal fighting blades, they were still plenty sharp enough for my purpose. Not to mention that their thick leather sheaths protected my thighs. It was for that reason that I also wore a broad bladed throwing dagger on the upper part of each arm.

Susa wore a similar body thong only without the metal reinforcements. Her lower arms were protected by a plain pair of leather bracers and her hands by an equally plain set of fingerless leather gloves. On her feet she wore her normal knee length black leather boots with a 4 inch spiked heel. A 'gift' from an admirer, the boots were enchanted to ease her movement so that she could run and leap as if she was wearing flats. While I wouldn't admit it to her, I've always been a bit envious of those boots and have kept an eye open for a pair.

For weapons Susa took just her Coven blade. But her real weapons were her spells. Susa was a warlock, a magical practitioner who gained her powers by making a deal with more powerful darker powers. The Coven blade was a large punch dagger that was the physical expression of that contract. While Susa could channel spells without the dagger their power was increased when she used it.

Susa had made the deal after she had escaped from a goblin slave camp. She had gotten away clean, but made the deal to free the other slaves still held within the camp. One of those other slaves had been my sister Gwen.

While the coven granted her tremendous powers that allowed her to quite literally turn her enemies to ash, it came with a harsh price. Other spell casters channel their powers through complex mental constructs or by sheer force of their personalities. Warlocks channel the magic energies they wield directly through their bodies. The side effects of this channelling are twofold. First they cause what Gwen calls 'psychic wounds' to appear on her body. The other side effect is pain, and from what Gwen has told me, a lot of pain. Susa has admitted to 'slight discomfort' when casting really powerful spells. But I know from other experience that Susa has a massively high tolerance for pain so I tend to believe Gwen's opinion as to how much pain Susa goes through while casting.

Finally ready for our break in, we travelled out to the stables where the other two black bitches were also getting ready for tonight's rescue.

Gwen is a strawberry blonde half-Elf, with green eyes that while not as dark as mine can look right past any mask you may have and directly into your soul. At 5'3" tall Gwen is about the average height for a human female in the City of Gates but her lean frame leans more towards Elven proportions than human. Except for the breasts which are round and Humanly pert. This mixing of the best features of both Elves and Humans is the chief reason why so many are envious of half-Elves.

My half-sister; Gwen, is a cleric to the Lightbearer, aka the Sun God, Protector of Common Man, the Summer God, and for reasons I've yet to figure out, the Truth Seeker. Gods are big on titles and little on actual names. He is often seen as a wimpy God in the City of Gates, being the only 'Good' god that's openly allowed to be worshipped in the city. But there is no denying the strength of the Lightbearer's cleric's healing magic; nor can Gwen's courage be denied. She talks about how he dictates to his followers to always strive to 'bring light into the dark places'. Well, all I know is that when something truly bad happens in this city, it's the Lightbearer's holy people that are first on the scene. Either helping the survivors or dealing with the problem directly. Because they ask for no payment in return and expect no favours, they're seen by many as the biggest suckers in the city. Hells they don't even blackmail donations out of people before they heal them.

Being a cleric of such an upright and naïve deity, you wouldn't normally expect someone like Gwen to be working with such a roguish (some would use the word slutty) group. But family ties are important to my sister, so she willingly pitches in whenever she can. According to her, so as long as no one can absolutely prove she was ever involved in 'questionable' activities, the church turns a blind eye to her 'missionary' work.

When Gwen does work with us she exchanges her plain simple robes for a short hauberk of black chainmail with leather boots and a black leather half mask that keeps her face hidden from view. While the chain is heavy for the City's climate (at least in my opinion) Gwen swears by it, saying that unlike the rest of us leaping around the battlefield like a bunch of dance students, she just stands in one place and use her divine magic to get the job done.

Standing beside her, getting a heavy layer of bear fat smeared across her body was my other Elven sister Lia. Lia and Gwen had the same Elf mother. Gwen's father was also my father. So both Lia and I are Gwen's half-sisters while neither of us is directly related to each other. But Gwen found both of us after Susa's rescue from the goblins, calling us both family and declaring all three of us sisters. At first Lia and I just went along to humour this high energy force of a God. But since that time we have grown close and we also consider ourselves sisters. Of course this hasn't stopped the occasional hook up on our part. I mean who wouldn't want to? Lia is hot.

At 4'10" and maybe 75 pounds Lia is petite even for an Elf. She was raised in the city's slums where food was scarce and small girls often go hungry. To survive, Lia learned that a quick tongue and a quicker pair of hands could get you as far as a strong right arm. With long golden blonde hair and equally golden eyes, Lia also learned quickly how to play the dumb blonde pretty girl to the T. But she isn't dumb: Lia's a skilled acrobat and contortionist who specializes in getting into places that most thought impossible, stealing the valuables in there and getting out again. Now in her late teens, Lia's reputation as a thief was known by only an elite few, but those that do respect her for both her skills and her ruthlessness.

Tonight the plan was for Lia to enter the Hector house through the drains. She had done this several times before with other homes and was confident that she could do it there. It would be a tight fit however, hence beside the grease she was dressed in only a G-string. A leather cord 6 feet long was tied around her waist leading to our magical bag of holding that was our salvation. Our most obvious magical item, it held all of our main weapons and armour, healing potions, drug neutralizers and a hundred other small items so that we could make our getaway.

"Finally, we've been waiting forever!" Lia said, upon seeing Susa and me.

"Sorry, but it takes time to figure out what to wear to your own capture and interrogation," said Susa.

"You two ready?" I asked.

"As we'll ever be, I'm still not sure about this plan, it still feels crazy to me," replied Gwen as she attempted to remove the excess fat from her hands.

"It is crazy," I said. "Crazy like a fox; it will work just you wait."

"I've been meaning to ask you something. What exactly is a fox?" questioned Lia.

I stopped for a second, lost in thought. I had to admit it was one of my favourite phrases, but I wasn't really sure.

"It's a kind of wild dog that's known for its cleverness and difficulty to hunt," replied Susa.

"Oh, so it's a good thing to be crazy like that then. I wasn't sure," said Lia optimistically.

# Chapter Two

The plan called for us to get near the wooded wall of the Hector estate. After making sure that Lia was safely away in the drains, Gwen slowly drove by the Hector's estate wall opposite to the main gate. Susa and I got out there. Sixty minutes from now, Gwen would drive to the front gate in her Lightbearer church robes innocently asking directions, and talk her way into staying there until we came out.

After letting us off, Susa and I were able to scale the wall fairly easily. While not in Lia's league, both of us are good at keeping hidden. However, we were surprised by just how deep into the estate we were able to get before anyone seemed to have noticed. We were halfway down a passageway between the inner courtyard and the cellars when both ends of the passageway filled with armed guards.

It would have been easy to surrender there and then, but Susa and I had reputations to keep up. So in a flash of leather and steel, we ran at the guards between us and freedom. But the guards only fell back into the courtyard where ten times as many guards were waiting, out of melee range but point blank for the crossbows that many were armed with.

Standing back to back, both of us stood ready for whatever counter attack they had planned for us. We heard rather than saw the iron portcullis slam down behind us. I felt Susa stiffen, knowing that whatever was going to happen, it was going to happen soon.

We didn't wait long: a whirlwind sprung up around us,

it swiftly grew strong enough to suck the air from our lungs; it lifted us off our feet then flung us to the ground.

As suddenly as the whirlwind rose, it ended. Looking up, my mouth became suddenly dry as I saw a dozen sharp spear heads pointed right at me.

It was then that I heard the high reedy laughter and I knew that they had been waiting for us all along.

"Oh great," Susa muttered. "The bitch is here."

Sure enough, Storm came out from between two guards. Storm was a sorceress and a Dark Elf, neither of which would endear her to many within the Compact. Sorcerers are powerful spellcasters who control their magic through shear willpower and the force of their personalities. The personality that can direct magic, though simple, will tend to be a stubborn domineering type. Not the kind that play well with a Compact Noble who simply thinks that just because they are paying for everything that they actually can give the orders. Then of course there is the fact that she's a Dark Elf, and a Dark Elf female to boot. And no one trusts Dark Elves, generally seeing them as conniving, vicious backstabbing thieves. The women are even worse, believing that just because they're women they can actually run things.

Storm however is the exception: she has the reputation of being a rule bender, not a rule breaker. Also she can work reasonably well with others, and leave everyone on her side alive until the end of her contract. It also doesn't hurt that she's been blessed with more than her share of Elven beauty: The skank. Storm's height and bearing clearly mark her as dark Elf nobility. What I always note first about Storm is her solid red fey eyes. High Elves, Gnomes, Dark Elves, doesn't matter, those unicolour eye just drive me nuts. I think it's because I find them so hard to read, like talking to someone with a hood on. However, the Dark Elf's clothing left little that needed translation.

Wearing a half coat which left much of her midriff

bare, a black silk thong, black stockings and a pair of black fuck-me pumps, all covered in intricate silver embroidery, Storm didn't so much ooze sexual desire as flood the area with it. Keeping up the 'all Dark Elves are sluts' stereotype must take so much work. On her shoulder rested a tiny silver dragon familiar that looked down at Susa and me with what could only be described as a lustful eye.

As she approached, I saw that in her left hand was a silvery blue curved dagger while in the other was a flat grey one. The weapons glowed with magical energy and I knew the weapons performed much the same role for Storm as did Susa's Coven blade. "Get them," she said.

With that, eight of the biggest guards came forward with ropes and gags and clubs. Before I could get up, they had me face down. I could have broken away from 2 guards, maybe 3, but not 4, and my hands and feet were soon bound. I was still in my armour though, that was a good sign. Susa tried to utter a spell, but one of the guards drove a short club with all his weight behind it into her solar plexus, knocking the wind out of her.

While Susa was still trying to get a breath, she was gagged, blindfolded and bound. "Damn you Storm you don't have to be so rough!" I shouted helplessly.

"Oh but I do, the warlock's tongue is sharper than steel. There will be no spells uttered here," said the Dark Elf as she knelt before me. Then, sliding her hand underneath my armour she gave my right breast a hard squeeze. "Don't worry, Blood Princess, you'll be singing prettily enough for both of you soon enough," said Storm with a smile. "Get them to the theatre," She said, turning to the guards. Then in a blur of silk and clack of heels on cobblestones she was gone.

We were then bundled up over a couple of the guards' shoulders and carried to 'the theatre.'

# Chapter Three

Disturbingly enough, the 'theatre' turned out to be an actual full-sized theatre: it had worn stone seating, solid wood flooring, and excellent resonance. Around 20 bored Compact family members of various ages and an equal number of servants sat in the stands enjoying the opening act. Unfortunately, it appeared that the style of performance the theatre specialized in was torture.

Much of the apparatus I recognized from Brutal's dungeon: chains, whips, a couple of different racks, two 'performance' benches, a wild pony with a metal edge, and a crow picker. All these implements of pain were cheerily lit by magical spot lights. The major difference between here and Brutal's place of work was that he kept equipment extremely clean and well maintained; with padded cuffs so that the actual equipment didn't add any effects that Brutal did not want. In this theatre however, while the equipment was maintained after a fashion blood and other fluids were still present, as well all the manacles and binding devices had sharp or rough edges with only added to the subject's discomfort.

In front of all these torture devices were the Aster twins, providing the bottom component to the warm-up act. Pale-skinned with the best bodies that magic could modify, the two teenagers were the jewels in the Aster crown. But they weren't being treated like jewels now: both were naked, their flawless skin sheened in sweat, forced to kneel each with one knee between the other's legs so that each of their sexes rested on her sister's thigh. The slightest movement of either would cause her to hump the other's leg. Their arms were bound above their heads, with a set of manacles running down from the ceiling, while metal hoops bound their ankles to the floor. Their wrist bindings were set high enough that the twins' thighs could not rest on their calves, forcing them to choose between resting their full weight upon their bound wrists or to try to take some of the weight with their legs. As a final cruel twist, the torturer had joined the girls' nipples together for constant nipple play with a single piercing ring for each set of perfect breasts. They couldn't stay in one place and squirmed helplessly in their bonds, twisting their naked bodies from position to position, every move grinding their pussies against the other's leg; each girl's thigh was coated in cum from her sister's climaxes, their writhing naked bodies, and their hoarse cries as they were whipped and came brought the audience their entertainment.

But the Aster twins were not the only actors in the performance: walking around the two was a half-naked Elf overseer carrying a long bullwhip. She divided her time between providing a commentary to the crowd in Elfish and encouraging the twins to do their bit in the act: they whimpered and cried, sweat standing out on their flesh, drops of it pouring down their naked skin to drop to the floor and mingle with the puddles of their girl cum pooling about their legs; the air was pungent with the odour of stale sweat and female arousal as they squirmed helplessly in their bonds, their voices rising toward yet another climax. Looking at them and the welts on their backs breaking their flawless skin, they must have been entertaining for some time now.

Trying to find the silver lining in the situation I thought: *Okay, part one and part two of the plan is complete. Now we just have to hope that Lia could find us quickly so that we could get out of here.* I was not able to dwell on cheery hope for any length of time. The whole scene seemed to be overseen by a Minotaur. Close to 7 feet tall and dressed in a loin cloth, leather apron and an air of command, he bellowed at our guards and pointed to a table centre stage. Susa and I were unceremoniously dumped onto the table by the guards, who stood back, waiting for orders.

Staring up, I saw a large mirror angled so that the audience could clearly see Susa and I. In return of course we could clearly see them. We had expected interrogation and torture, but I doubt even Susa expected the interrogation to be done for the entertainment of a group of bored compact nobles.

For a while though, nothing happened; the Minotaur continued to prepare something in the corner. Only once he was done did the large beastman approach us. As he did so I heard a round of polite applause as the twins' act was ended. They were released and moved off front stage. Apparently we were the next act.

Without a word, the horned torturer took up what looked like pruning shears that he used to cut away our armour. The only items spared the shears were Susa's gag and blindfold and, not surprisingly, her boots. Those he deftly took off and put to the side. Throughout, the audience kept up with a steady stream of cat calls along with the occasional ooohs or ahhs: I guess they liked what they saw.

Once he was done with stripping us both, he replaced our rope bindings with metal shackles binding our wrists to our ankles, forces our legs to stay open. Finally, he took a narrow metal choker and buckled it it around Susa's neck. It glowed pale blue for a moment, then appeared to become even tighter.

Once that was done, the beast finally spoke. "Alright bitches, listen up," he said, projecting his voice to the audience. "My name is Jak and I'm the theatre director, so my word is law." He slapped Susa across one breast to get her attention and said. "The choker around your neck has been magiced so that if *any* arcane power is used it will start to tighten on its own. It won't stop tightening until it cuts your head off. Understand?"

Susa nodded understanding.

"The good news is that I can take the gag off now," he said bluntly, removing the gag and blindfold.

Bewildered at first, Susa quickly got her bearings. Looking up and spotting the mirror she only sighed as if she was more disappointed than frightened by the situation we found ourselves in.

Her disapproval was lost upon Jak who started to rub us down with olive oil to remove the black ash from our bodies. The audience fell silent, giving him their complete attention as he ran a cloth over our naked skin. I couldn't hold back a gasp as his fingers crept over me, finding every pleasure and pain spot; I tried to resist, but I couldn't help but cry out and groan; I felt Susa beside me tremble, her own voice raised in helpless cries as he worked on her.

He crept into the folds of our pussies, the smooth motion of his fingers rubbing over our clits; he swiped his cloth over our breasts, dragging it across our hardened nipples; his fingers familiar with every inch of the female body, and now with ours.

By the time the 'inspection' was over, both Susa and I were aroused and panting. The audience gave him a round of applause showing their appreciation for the result; they seemed pleased with both our condition and reaction.

"Excellent responsive fuck meat, Blood Princess," he said. "But then Brutal always does superior work even if he's a bit of a pansy; always going on about how the sub is the one truly in control. Control my ass. Who has the whip has the control." He gave me a hard slap on my ass to illustrate his point. "I do not recognize the training on you warlock. Who was your master?" he asked Susa with a note of professional curiosity.

"My Mistress' name is Liltha and you two don't share

the same plane of existence," Susa said contemptuously.

This got her a slap across the face from Jak, his heavy hand breaking Susa's lip. Susa rolled with the punch and first looked back at Jak then turned to the audience.

"I win," she said, letting her voice carry, a hungry smile on her face.

This caused the assembled compact members to laugh. Apparently few got one over the 'theatre director'

*Great, now she's playing to the audience*, I thought to myself, rolling my eyes.

The Minotaur looked as if he wanted to do more but he restrained himself, then he smiled cruelly. "We have to pause the preparations until all the commodities are present," he said. The audience was audibly disappointed by the news.

"However, I believe that Cecile is always looking for a fresh challenge," he said playing to the crowd.

So with the cheers and cat calls of the crowd ringing in our ears, Susa and I were bound into the apparatus that was still warm with the twin's body heat. Cecile's last step was to connect our tits together for the nipple play component. But instead of simply tying our rings together, Cecile ran a sharp curved needle down through the top of Susa's nipple, manoeuvred it through and up into the bottom of mine. With a hiss of pain we watched as with a simple command word from Cecile the ends of needles closed, pulling our already hard tits together.

"Ooo yes, make the sluts bleed Cecile! Whip them hard enough to rip their tits off!" screamed one over-active girl from the audience.

Thus began our turn at 'hump the cunt'. Cecile pulled back and started her slow walk around us. At first she wanted to gauge endurance so she kept her whip strikes to near misses hoping the sound and air movement would illicit the desired response.

Susa and I had both been in far more uncomfortable

situations, some of which were entirely voluntary on our parts, so we largely ignored the Elf. I took the time to test our bonds. Pulling down on the chains I felt some give and figured that I could break the links with one hard pull. Susa deciding upon a plan hung her full 90 lbs off the manacles to get her lips level with mine. She then gave me a passionate kiss followed by a nuzzling of neck. I also felt her hips start a circular pattern on my thigh as started to hump my naked flesh.

"Let's give these fuckers what they want," Susa whispered hoarsely in my ear. I recognized the heat in her voice and knew that she had lost herself in the sexual potential of the situation. "It will buy us more time than resisting."

It was right about then that Cecile decided to actually land a blow with the bull whip. The loud crack of leather against skin sounded as she landed her blow across Susa's shoulder blades.

The little warlock didn't even flinch. Instead she turned her head with an annoyed look at the Elf. "Do you mind?" she said. "I'm trying to get off here and you're breaking my rhythm."

Susa then went back to her grinding.

Both Cecile and the audience were taken aback by Susa's retort. The audience replied with laughter, Cecile with anger; apparently she wasn't used to dealing with bossy slaves. I could see her deciding that I was next.

What the hells, I'm a masochist not a submissive. Two can play at this game as well as one.

When the whip cracked across my lower back I admit I was under whelmed. I mean seriously, Brutal's warm up blows were harder.

"Next time could you try and get between my shoulder blades? I have an itch there that's really distracting," I said to the increased laughter of the crowd.

It was then my turn to nip and nuzzle Susa so that I

could whisper something.

"Is that choker for real? That seems like pretty powerful magic," I asked before I groaned in pleasure; Susa's gyrations were heating me up as well.

"As far as I can tell, yes it is for real, I'd maybe be able to get one of my quick spells off before it kills me but that would be iffy," she said.

"What about your ribs? That shot the guard gave you was pretty hard," I asked concerned.

"Bruised only; it's tender but nothing broken. I've gotten worse from Gwen when I steal the sheets," she replied. We then kissed with growing passion.

I then started to grind my own sex into the Warlock's leg. With practised ease I focused on the sensations that the movement provided. I then pulled back hard on my trapped nipples. Using the pain it generated to overload my body so it could only register the increased sensations I entered what in the City is known as 'slave space'. A place where your body becomes so stimulated, that you can no longer tell if the stimulation is coming from pleasure or pain.

About that time Susa pitched forward in her first climax of the night.

Cecile looked mad enough to spit nails. Both of her slaves were doing exactly what she wanted but they were completely ignoring her. She proceeded to lay into both of us with a series of what I'm sure were meant to be painful lashes from the whip, but she lacked both the skill and the strength to do more than add sensation to our already over-stimulated bodies.

How long we continued like that I wasn't really sure. We proceeded at our own pace ignoring the mistress. Yet we were providing the audience of compact nobles with a show the likes of which they've rarely seen. How many times either of us climaxed I wasn't sure but in the end Cecile had given up all control. Instead she matched her lashes with the whip to our rhythm in an attempt to give the illusion of that she was causing them.

Finally the performance was ended when the two of us were hit by a blast of ice cold water. The near freezing liquid pulled me back to reality so hard, that I pulled on the chains that held our hands above our heads with enough force to break that weak link.

Sputtering and looking around for the source of the water, I saw Jak standing 5 feet away with a magical decanter that had just stopped spraying us with its endless contents.

Besides him stood Storm, looking alarmed by the fact that Susa and I were suddenly half free. The guards that were escorting her levelled their spears at us.

I held up Susa and mine still manacled hands, to show we were still bound. The audience was complaining loudly about having their show interrupted. Jak held up a hand indicating a request for quiet and remarkably the nobles complied. "Enjoying showing off your depravity?" asked the Dark Elf.

"Not really, I don't usually like to perform in public unless I'm being paid for it," replied Susa before I could say anything.

"Where's Lia?" asked Storm ignoring Susa's retort.

"Who?" I asked before Susa could say anything.

"Don't play dumb with me Blood Princess you're not smart enough to do it well. Where is Lia, your golden haired thief?"

"It was her time of the month and she cramps really bad so she stayed home for this one," replied Susa without pausing.

"Susa, don't embarrass Lia like that!" I said, shocked. "What, we're all girls here, it's nothing that we all haven't talked about before," she replied, eyeing the guards. One of whom was actually blushing. Gods above, men and their phobias about women's periods.

"Where is she?" asked Storm again, anger filling her

voice.

"We don't know," I replied again.

Storm turned to Jak and said "They're lying. Use whatever means you choose to make them talk, but no permanent damage." Jak grunted acknowledgement. Then, motioning to the guards to help, he removed us from the rest of our bindings. As we stood we received a standing ovation from the Compact nobles. Susa, not missing a beat, curtsied, before allowing the guards to escort her back to the benches. As she turned I saw that her back was a solid pink with several welts severe enough to break the skin. As I recovered from the slave space I started to feel my own back's pain and figured that it most likely didn't look much better. But I'd be damned if I was going to let these bastards know how it hurt.

# Chapter Four

Once we were returned to the table, Jak once again chained us wrist to ankle although this time he left us on our stomachs.

"Hey you all here?" whispered Susa to me as the theatre director turned his back to us and addressed the crowd.

"Yeah. Yeah, I'm here," I replied, a little shakily; that cold water had jolted me out of slave space hard.

"Good; try not to go so far down next time. If they had asked the questions before the cold water you may have given them the right answer," she said.

"Shhh, I want to hear what's going to happen next," I hissed trying to listen to Jak.

"So what shall we use for the interrogation?" He shouted the crowd.

"Rack them!" "Whip their skins off!" "Boiling water!" "Set up the rape racks and we'll deal with them!" were some of the replies our bloodthirsty audience gave.

Finally Jak held up a hand and silence once again descended upon the theatre. "Good suggestions all," he said finally. "Unfortunately as we are under orders to not do any permanent damage they are not exactly what we need." Frowning, he turned to Susa and me and, giving us a wink, turned back to the crowd and said: "How about we break them on the pony?"

This got a roar of approval from the crowd who thought it was a wonderful idea.

Turning his attention back to us the Minotaur grabbed up a set of pre-cut ropes and used them to bind our arms and legs; worn out by our ordeal, we could not stop him forcing us back to back and pressing our limbs together, binding them in place so they were intertwined. When he was done, the way we were bound forced us to spread our legs, exposing our open snatches. Satisfied with how he had bound us, Jak picked us both up as a single unit. Carrying us several yards without apparent effort in his huge hands, he plunked us both down hard onto the wild pony. Susa and I cried out helplessly as our pussies landed on the metal edge, and then he wheeled the Wild Pony device centre stage, once more beneath the mirror.

Brutal has had me ride a wild pony before, but only with a blunt wooden edge, never a sharp metal one. It's a classic lesser of two evils torture: either you grind your clit and pussy against the hard edge of the pony or your thighs burned from the effort of keeping them off the edge. The mock riding motion that is generated by your predicament is what gave the device its name.

But the Minotaur wanted to up the stakes even further: once we were on and he'd adjusted our pussies so that the clits rested right on the iron, he lowered two nooses and placed one around each of our necks. Susa visibly gulped as he pulled it tight. He pulled on the rope and she had to raise herself up; I could both see and feel through our bound limbs as she tightened the muscles in her thighs to raise her pussy off of the metal. She struggled for control as Jak turned to me, lowering the second noose over my head to pull it snug about my neck. I gurgled as the noose pulled tight, and raised myself on trembling thighs until it loosened enough for me to gasp a breath.

Satisfied with our predicament, Jak took three steps back and uncoiled the bull whip that hung from his hip. He swung it over his head a couple of times, then brought it down with a loud crack between Susa and I. He did another crack right in front of my face and a third right in front of Susa. The fourth stroke he laid right across my stomach leaving a thin red welt. Unlike Cecile, Jak had both the skill and strength to use a whip correctly. I flinched forward and I dropped painfully down onto the edge, pulling Susa with me. We both gasped and warbled, struggling to raise ourselves up again as Jak coiled his whip again. "Where's the Elf?" he asked in a bored tone.

"I don't know," I gasped.

Jak just shrugged and started again with the cracking of the whip. This time it was once for me, twice for Susa. Only the little bitch didn't flinch: forewarned, she just took the hit and kept herself rigid.

Minutes that seemed like hours passed for Susa and me as fire burned in our pained thighs, as Jak lashed our bodies, all the while gasping for air as the nooses around our throats stayed tight.

Panting for breath, we lifted ourselves with our thighs high enough that we could breathe and relieve the pain on our clits and pussy lips. After several seconds however, the burning in our legs became so great we had to lower ourselves or fall, dropping back down onto the metal blade while the nooses tightened again.

Jak kept up his questions as he lashed us, still sounding bored as hell; he could keep this up all day, his tone and body language said, but his strength and skill with the whip never slackened. He used the whip both fast and slow, sharp and, altering his rhythm as we altered ours, preventing us from entering that over stimulated high as we had done with Cecile.

I groaned haplessly as we rose again off of the blade. Trembling with pain and exertion, we gulped air as the nooses loosened that vital bit; only to collapse once again onto the horse's metal back, as one or both of us was overwhelmed by the pain in our thighs or a well place lash upon another part of our bodies. Pain then radiated out from our still aroused pussy lips into our bodies as the dull metal edge felt like it was cutting us in half. After perhaps a handful of seconds the pain in our thighs was lower than the pain in our cunts and we repeated the ride all over again.

All the while the audience hooted and hollered as we rode the pony. "Let see them cum on that!" I heard one shout. "The redhead's in enough pain but the black haired bitch looks like she's out for a morning jog!" said another.

Then I heard a voice I was really getting pissed with. "Well, it seems like you're not having the desired impact," Storm said as she came forward to more closely examine what was going on. "Well let's try something different," said the dark Elf. Adopting the uniform for a female torturer on Jak's stage, she had removed her jacket and stockings, and was now dressed only in a thong and Susa's boots (I guess she likes looking taller as well). I noticed that the Dark Elf's nipples were rock hard; she smiled at us, an aroused, delighted gleam in her eyes at the prospect of what she was about to do next.

Without a word she produced half a dozen long steel needles; she held them up in one hand for all to see as she walked up to us. She took one and held it in front of my eyes. My mouth suddenly went dry as I knew what she was going to do. Even with the foreknowledge, I screamed as she plunged the needle through my right breast, only stopping when it exited out the other side.

My thrashing caused the noose to tighten, cutting off my scream in a strangled gurgle, I heard Susa gagging and realized that my movement had broken our rhythm and she was paying for it as well.

"Annie calm down! Ride the pain through," the warlock gasped hoarsely through the tightening noose.

"Where is the thief?" asked the Dark Elf, holding another needle before my eyes.

"I don't know where she is," I gasped, struggling to hold myself up.

With a wicked smile, Storm plunged the needle

through my left breast.

I still screamed, shuddering in pain, fighting not to thrash and pull at Susa's bound and helpless body. Once I could, I glared hard at Storm. The sorceress just smirked back at me and turned toward Susa. She asked Susa the same question.

"Go fuck yourself!" Susa snapped.

The little spellcaster stiffened, hissing through her teeth. I then heard a hawking sound and then someone spiting. Nine Hells, Susa's pain tolerance was incredible. No bucking, no scream, just a whole shitload of attitude directed at her torturer.

Storm didn't say a thing but suddenly I felt a sharp pain lance through my clit and vulva lips. My entire body stiffened and I was unable to breath let alone scream or even move.

Then as soon as it had happened, it was over, and I could breathe again. "Metal channels lightening very well, you warlock bitch, keep that in mind," said Storm. Susa remained silent.

"I thought I left instructions that no permanent damage was to be done to any of the young ladies?"

Everyone stiffened at the sound of the voice: the audience, the guards, Jak, Storm, Hells even Susa and I.

There stood the creature that would be the focus of my nightmares for many years to come: Hector, lord of House Hector, one of the most powerful beings in the city. Looking at him, I saw a man in his mid-to-late 50s with perfectly cut grey hair, exceptional taste in clothing and impeccable poise standing at the top of the stairs leading down to the theatre. He was flanked by two guards in plate mail and full helms. Both were armed with the standard House Hector two handed spears, only these were made of solid metal. Hector himself was unarmed, but he still felt like the most dangerous man I'd ever been in the presence of. With a burst of shuffling, everyone in the room, the ones not already bound, either knelt or stood up and bowed before the man.

If I could have I'd have knelt before the man myself: suddenly I felt very self-conscious about my appearance. I very much wanted this man's approval as if he was the one and only person in the whole world whose opinion about me mattered.

"Forgive me Master Hector, but you also made it clear that finding the third girl was also vital. A simple healing potion will deal with the welts and punctures so no permanent harm has been done," said Storm carefully.

I had to admit I've seen wheedling but what Storm did was impressive; she almost had me convinced of her sincerity.

"That might be the case, but you certainly seem dressed to enjoy the situation. But from what I have seen, Dark Elves seem to think that showing off some tits will make anyone they talk to more malleable," said Hector in an almost parental tone. As he moved down the stairs, not so much taking the steps but flowing down them as if they were moving, not him. His bodyguards stayed where they were.

Once on the floor Hector came to stand in front of me.

"Ah, so this is the Blood Princess. A rather gaudy name for one so pretty," he said as he lifted my chin so that I looked him directly in the eyes.

"Tell me Princess, where is your Elf companion?" he asked such a simple question, and as I looked into his deep grey eyes it occurred to me that I really wanted to please Hector and that he'd be so happy with me if I just told him the truth.

"She doesn't know where Lia is; neither do I," said Susa interrupting Hector as he spoke to me.

I was so angry with her right then, Hector was asking *me*, damn it! He wanted *me* to answer the question, not Susa! Why did she have to butt in?

"Ah, the warlock finds her voice, does she? But you can wait while I finish talking to the Blood Princess," said Hector, his voice firm.

I was so pleased when Hector turned his attention back to me. I was the special one; I was the one whom he'd chosen to ask questions to. After staring into my eyes for several seconds he asked quietly "Where is your little thief?"

"She's in the sewers. She's to crawl through them and up into the house," I said, hoping to please him.

"Oh, why is she doing that?"

"Leave her alone, Vampire!" shouted Susa. It was strange because I was sure she was still bound to me but she sounded as if she was suddenly shouting over a great distance.

I then felt a sharp pain in the centre of my back as Susa dug her finger nails into my already wounded flesh leaving bleeding furrows.

The pain was like fire to me, its sudden shock forcing me back into the here and now, and away from whatever effect Hector had me under.

I heard a sharp crack of a hand on flesh. "Hector told you to be silent, bitch," Storm shouted, enraged.

"Is that the best you can do, Storm? You couldn't slap the flies from a horse's ass with a blow like that," said Susa, her mouth running off again. Storm growled and I heard her grab up something from the tray.

"Our fifth offering is in the sewers, Storm. Why don't you try to find her now that we've got the information that we wanted," suggested Hector. "Yes sir," replied Storm. I then saw her running past me putting her jacket back on as she headed up the stairs. With all of the attention off of me for a few seconds I was able to clear my head a bit.

Vampire! That's what Susa had said, and if she was right (and she usually was when it came to arcane stuff) then the bastard had been in my mind and made me tell him what he wanted to hear, right from the friggin' start.

Turning his attention back to me, Hector smiled his dazzling smile and suddenly I'd forgotten why I was angry with him.

"Thank you Blood Princess, you have been most helpful." He said, and I was so pleased that I was able to help.

Then as a reward he removed the needles from my breasts, licking the blood from them before setting them down onto the tray.

"Brand them Jak, and then force enough healing draughts into each of them so it looks like they've been marked since birth. That should cover over any other marks that are on them as well. I have to make sure that the final preparations for the gate to be opened are completely," said Hector to the Minotaur as he moved over to remove the needle from Susa's breast.

"Of course master, it shall be done as you ask. But what about our timeline; we are cutting it close,"

"We shall make our deadline, slave, not to worry. I will give our 'arcane expert' another hour, then I will talk to her about returning here for her part in all this."

He turned to Susa and me. "Ladies, we need to do more to prepare you for your journey; I look forward to seeing you in a few hours' time."

He then turned his stern gaze to the theatre audience. "Tonight is an important night for our House. I'm sure that we all have our roles to play tonight. Do we not?" he said, his voice firm by still pleasant.

There was a sudden flurry as the theatre emptied. He then turned back to the rest of us on stage with a brief look heavenwards, said, "Children." And then he was gone, flowing away the same way he had come in.

After he left, Jak left us still on the horse, which meant that we still faced the torture ride just to keep breathing. But at least we were alone for a minute as he moved towards the back of the theatre.

"Damn it, we were played," Susa gasped under her breath as we raised ourselves on shaking thighs.

"What?" I asked, still not fully recovered from the effects of Hector's voice.

"We. Were. Played!" Susa hissed. "This job was never about the twins. . . it was always about getting you and your *two* black bitches here!"

I was cogent enough to get Susa's emphasis on the fact that they hadn't figured out that Gwen was part of the team. "So we stall for time then?" I asked.

"Yeah, I can't see Storm and a bunch of house guards finding Lia." Susa tensed as I saw Jak coming back to us out of the corner of my eye. With practised ease, the huge horned male removed us from the wild pony and brought us back to the table. There he untied us from each other, but rebound our hands behind our backs. He then directed the remaining guards to escort us towards a large rack on the far side of the stage. I scanned the area looking for opportunities but the only big change I noticed was that Susa's devil tattoo was gone.

That tattoo is in fact her familiar Ordis. Normally he just 'sleeps' on Susa's shoulder blade, but when she needs him to be active, he peels off of her back and becomes a fully 3-dimensional Imp. The cocky little pervert also has the ability to turn invisible, and while I've never heard him communicate verbally (hand gestures he does just fine) Susa claims he can tell her a whole bunch of things.

During all the commotion Ordis must have gone active, which gave us one advantage that we didn't have before.

# Chapter Five

"So Jak, were the twins ever kidnapped in the first place?" asked Susa, as Jak sat us down on a rough wooden bench.

"No," Jak snorted. Minotaurs snort really well by the way. "You are all part of the tribute that must be paid in order to keep the Compacts fulfilled. The twins were just Aster's contribution. Being twins, they were marked as such since they were born," he added.

"Why us then? We're not Compact born, we're scum living off of Compact scraps," asked Susa

"Maybe you're a good fuck, I don't know," replied Jak. "You'd have to ask the Master that question. I just have to brand you with our mark and the year, so that your new owners remember we held up to our end of the contract."

Just the matter-of-fact way he said that caused my guts to roll over. I've been burned before, and cut, and crushed, and stabbed, you get the idea; oh the boring life of a freelancer. But everyone in the City of Gates fears to be branded: that's a slave's mark. Your life outside of the Compact might be harsh, but at least it's yours. Under Compact law a slave is owned, body and soul. You can be modified, bred, 'enhanced', dissected, killed and then resurrected all at your owner's whim. Even your soul is a commodity; both devils and demons will pay hard coin for a soul. And the penalty for anyone other than an owner to kill or harm a slave? Well, that's destruction of private property, a small fine.

"You're branding us as a hedge against breach of contract?" asked Susa.

"Yeah, I guess so," replied Jak with a bored shrug.

Susa just shook her head. Even for someone as jaded to life as the warlock was, this was a new Compact low. Without saying anything further, Jak got started. He picked up Susa and put her down on her stomach on the rack. Two of the attending guards responded to Jak's order to shackle her down, wrapping the cold steel manacles around her ankles and wrists, and then Jak placed his hands on the rack's wheels and turned it. With the immense strength of his massive shoulders and thick arms, he slowly turned the wheel, drawing the chains tight; Susa grunted and tugged against the manacles as they hauled on her arms and legs, but she couldn't stop her limbs from straightening out, then stretching out; she grunted, her pale skin gleaming with sweat as Jak secured the rack, then the torturer grabbed a leather gag and held it to Susa's mouth. She couldn't resist his overwhelming strength, and the Minotaur shoved it into place between Susa's teeth. Without a word being spoken, he took out a long brush and painted Susa's right butt cheek with a glowing silvery substance.

That's when I knew they were serious: the silvery liquid is known as glow silver (yes, I know, not very original but it apparently sounds way cooler in Elvish) Glow silver allows the shape of the brand to be magically altered, to allow sales between owners, but it prevents the brand being removed through any means, even magical healing.

The final preparations done, the two guards put their hands and weight on Susa, while Jak strode to a burning furnace and lifted out a white-hot iron. I could do nothing but stare in horror as Jak approached the young woman holding the branding iron before him. Susa trembled, watching him come near, and finally broke; she screamed into her gag, bucking and squirming in her bonds, panic and fear ruling her as her naked body was flung about. But the two guards and her tight bonds held her, and Jak lowered the iron to her right butt cheek, and her scream rose yet higher, her sweat-sheened body rigid as hot fiery pain plunged through her helpless body. Jak pressed the iron into her hard for a good thirty seconds, and Susa's scream lasted through the whole time, tears of pain, horror and fear pouring from her eyes.

Finally it was done. Jak pulled back with the iron to inspect the mark that he had made, eyeing her marked ass with a businesslike air, ignoring the pitiful whimper Susa uttered, her body heaving with sobs as she cried. "The Dark Elf was right," Jak said. "Her hide is as tough as a dragon's when it comes to fire" he said, in a businesslike manner.

I winced; somehow, somewhere Susa had become immune to normal fires. It was one of the reasons she was as pale as a ghost; the sun couldn't tan her.

As the guards released Susa, Jak removed the remaining glow silver from the branding area with a cloth that he took from a silvery box at the side of the table. Only once he had returned did he reach down to remove the gag from Susa's mouth. He had to pry it free, her teeth had become locked around it in the throes of pain.

She took a breath, a sick wheeze, and hung her head in shame; she was no longer a person, in the Compact, but property.

Jak released her from the manacles binding her to the rack, but there was no release from her new bonds of slavery. I'd seen Susa hurt before, but I could see a real terrible shock in her tear-streaked eyes as he escorted her back to where the remaining guards held me. She shuffled along, hurt in body and spirit, broken, perhaps forever; I stared at her in concern as the guards bound her hands behind her back, but she didn't meet my gaze.

And then it was my turn. I guess Jak suspected that I would try something, given that I'm much stronger than Susa and known as a nasty close-in fighter. Before I knew what was happening, one of the guards nailed me from behind with a sucker punch.

I regained my senses as the padded gag was being shoved between my teeth. I was already chained to the wrack, my arms and legs strained by the tight chains; I could feel my spine stretch as the rack pulled on every fiber of my body. The brush wiped over my right butt cheek, and I pulled hard on the chains; I knew it was futile, but I couldn't help myself. I panicked, struggling wildly when I saw Jak walking towards me with a red-hot branding iron.

"Your lover over there says that you're normal when it comes to fire and heat. This will be much shorter for you than for her," Jak said reassuringly.

I stared up at him and whimpered pleadingly.

Then he branded me.

I screamed. I screamed so loud that I thought that I would rupture something. It felt like it was burning a hole into my skin forever.

Then it was over, I felt the iron taken from my body, but the burn still throbbed, masking the pain of my cuts on my wrists and ankles from where I had tried to break free from the shackles. Jak called the four guards who brought me over and they held me down as I was unchained from the rack and then rebound to be taken back to the bench where Susa still sat.

I fell onto the bench beside her, and she glance at me; I caught her eye, but there were no words to say.

One of the guards came over with a flask for each of us. "It's a powerful healing potion that will remove all of your injuries," he said. I mentally shrugged as he raised it to my lips, and opened my mouth wide to let him pour it down my throat. I gulped it down, in too much pain and too low to care. Almost before I took the last of it I felt better, a whole lot better as the euphoria of suddenly not being in pain kicked in. I looked down at myself, then over at Susa: our welts from the whip, the punctures from Storm's needles, and the cuts from the manacles were just gone. I looked down at Susa's brand, and while still there it was healed, as if the branding had occurred months ago.

The brand itself was interesting: about three inches by four, it bore House Hector's seal, but below that was lettering like I'd never seen before. I didn't have time to examine it closely as the guards grabbed us by our bound arms escorted us off-stage. There we found the twins in a narrow cage clearly meant only for one person.

"Your turn m'ladies," one of guards said with a cruel flourish as the twins were hauled out to be branded. Once the cage was empty Susa was forced in, and I unceremoniously dumped in on top of her; Susa groaned as my weight fell on her smaller body, then the guards slammed the door shut and locked it, then they left us there.

There was little room to manoeuvre in the cage but we struggled, bound as we were, to get as comfortable as we could, our naked skin sliding. Once we lay beside each other, we sulked. Neither Susa nor I was in a good head space to talk. We just lay there in silence, listening to the Aster twins scream as our two contracts joined us in slavery.

Once those faded away there was only silence between us. So we had plenty of opportunity to hear the drill break through the wood near our heads.

I twisted my neck, turning my head, I stared incredulously as first one then two small hearing bells poked through an inch wide hole in the wooden floor.

"About time," Lia's voice drifted through one of the bells. "Hells you two have a set of lungs on you."

"Lia, am I glad that you're here!" I whispered, feeling a faint spark of hope; together again, we stood a chance. "We've been played: the twins were just bait, we were the target all along. They're planning on shipping us to another plane as part of some trade agreement." I frowned as something else occurred to me. "How the Hells are you under us anyways?"

"They have a storage area under the stage I was able to get into," Lia said. "Your performances on the wild pony kept everyone focused on you so it was easy to slip in and under. With that Dark Elf skank looking for me this is really the safest place. So, what's next?

"We need to get out of here, but how in the Nine Hells we're supposed to do that I don't have a fucking clue," started Susa with growing frustration. "I always thought that this was a minor tit for tat thing between the two houses, you know, small time stuff. But with Hector himself involved we're talking the full resources of the house are at work, with him being a Vampire and a very old one at that. . ." Susa's voice trailed away to nothing; Susa is very smart, don't get me wrong, but often she overwhelms herself with ideas and becomes paralyzed, especially in crunch situations.

That's fine, because that's where I shine.

Slipping my thigh between her legs, I moved my head as if I was nuzzling her neck, so that both she and Lia could listen to my idea. But for anyone just watching it looked as if we were at it again. (And this is how you get a rep as a complete, slut by the way) "Is your little creep in a place where he can give us a warning if someone is starting to get too interested?" I asked Susa.

"Yeah," she whispered back. "Ordis is right beside us admiring your brand."

"Did not need to know that," I ground out between gritted teeth. Calming down, I continued. "The way we get out of here is through a distraction. Something that is big enough that Hector has to deal with it instead of with us," I went on. "Now, Hector said he's opening an independent portal to get to wherever. Susa, I remember you saying once that those kinds of rituals take a lot of time, and lot of prep to do. And if someone interrupts the process it can be very bad, right?"

"Oh very, very bad, and a very large distraction," she

said, starting to get the idea.

"Lia, do you think Gwen could get through the drains?" I asked. "We're dealing with a vampire here; a cleric of the Sun God would be a real help."

"Yeah I think so. She may lose a few layers of skin, but yeah I can get her in," she said.

"Alright," I said. "This is what I propose. . ."

# Chapter Six

It took fifteen minutes to get the plan laid out. Once we were done, Lia disappeared back into the darkness. Now it was just a matter of time for House Hector to further its plans.

It took only another half an hour for the final act of Hector's grand scheme to start; he arrived back in the theatre, just as Storm did, and she went up to him bowing at the waist. "I'm sorry, sir; your men were unable to locate the Elf," she said. "I've posted guards at all the entrances within the compound that we could find, but there is no guarantee that she had not just escaped back into the city's lines. She could be anywhere by now," Storm added, with a surprising degree of humility.

"Oh, that's alright my dear, sometimes these things happen," old Hector replied. "When you get as old as I, you appreciate the unexpected things even when they're bad news." While it wasn't directed at me this time, I could still feel the tug of his words upon me. That man's voice and presence; all he needed to do was focus his attention on you and you were his. "But be that as it may, you helped deliver two of the three tributes to us. For that I would like to add this gift to the payment we agreed to," Hector said, his voice still pleasant, still cordial. He handed her a choker the exact same style as the one that Susa currently wore.

"Thank you my lord, this is a most unexpected gift," said Storm, genuinely pleased that Hector deemed her worthy of such largesse.

"Try it on," he suggested.

Without even thinking, Storm put it on and stood there

looking up to see what she could do next.

Hector motioned to Jak and the Minotaur quickly grabbed the Dark Elf by the arms, dragging her hands together behind her back. "Hey, what's going on; what are you doing?" she cried out, as she came to her senses and realized something was very wrong. But too late; Jak easily bound her hands together with tight leather cords, despite her useless struggles; Storm kicked and squirmed, her body writhing helplessly in the Minotaur's grasp.

"It never occurred to you that you'd be just as good tribute as The Blood Princess and her companions?" Hector asked. "A Dark Elf spellcaster, and a high noble no less; you were always a backup in case one died or was deemed inappropriate."

The vampire then turned to his 'theatre director' "Jak, the harem matrons are coming to make the tributes presentable. Make sure that this one is branded and ready for them," he said pointing at Storm.

"It shall be all as you wish, master," replied Jak, bowing low, still keeping Storm still in his hands.

As Hector departed, Jak grabbed what little Storm was wearing and tore it away. "No!" Storm screamed, kicking her legs uselessly. "No, stop!" she cried out as the Minotaur lifted her in his arms and carried her over to the rack. Her screams rose higher, echoing throughout the theatre when the hot iron kissed her right butt cheek. I couldn't suppress a shiver at her cries, remembering the feel of the hot iron on my own soft flesh.

The guards released Storm from the rack and forced healing potions down her throat. They then dragged her over to the other side of the stage, where the twins had been secured against the wall. As they bound her beside them, a gaggle of older women and male slaves entered the theatre.

Susa and I were dragged out of our cage and given into the hands of what I guessed were the harem matrons. A large tub of piping hot water was brought in by the male slaves. All of us tributes were dumped into the water and the matrons proceeded to scrub the dirt, grime blood, and other dried fluids, along with three layers of skin, off of us.

Once washed, we were each tied to stiff backed chairs with soft but strong silk rope. As we sat bound there, the servants styled our hair, applied makeup, and finally perfume. As a final touch, the matrons added jewellery. Bracelets, rings, arm and leg bands, even new body piercings to enhance our otherwise naked bodies. I couldn't really see myself, but Susa looked hotter than the ninth plane of Hell: her jet black hair curled and cascading down her back in an obsidian waterfall, silver pins gleaming in the dark curls like stars. Her other jewellery was also silver inset with onyx, the black stone contrasting with her pale complexion but matching her eyes.

In my case the matrons went with gold jewellery, with chips of ruby. The most expensive piece was the finger nail-sized ruby that was affixed through my navel.

"Well these old ladies know what works; I've never seen you look sexier. Or more the Blood Princess without being covered in blood," said Susa, looking me over with an appraising eye. Lia finding us and then me coming up with a plan that at, least on the surface, gave us a fighting chance of getting out of here alive had helped Susa and I to feel a little cocky once again.

Once the matrons were done, our hands were once more bound behind our backs with the silk ropes. A dozen Hectorite elite guards (in scale mail, with heavy two handed spears) escorted the five of us deeper into House Hector's grounds, to what seemed to be the estate's central gardens. We were the last to arrive, finding another half dozen elite guards, six older house members and Hector with his two plate mail-clad bodyguards already there as we entered.

The gardens themselves were a wonder. Fifty feet to a side, it was full of flowering plants and bushes. The heady smell was almost overpoweringly sweet in the cool air of the night.

"Must be Hector's private garden," Susa observed quietly. "Who else would want a garden that flowers only at night?"

Along the side of each wall were a series of embedded glow stones, but what light they normally gave off was overwhelmed by what glowed in the centre of the garden.

The interdimensional gate through which our new lives were supposed to start stood there, crackling with energy, gleaming silver-white as bright as the sun.

Now for those who did not grow up in The City of Gates and haven't seen interdimensional gates as a matter of daily routine, let me dispel a few false assumptions: first off, world gates are not always open. The physical gate is nothing more than a storage point for the energy that will then be used to force open the weak point in-between the two dimensions that is the gate itself. (Don't be so surprised by me knowing this. Growing up in this city you just absorb it)

The second thing is that not all gates are round in shape: I've seen squares, rectangles, and hexagrams along with circles.

This gate was a triangle with energy gathering points along the length of the vertical sides. Inscribed on the ground was a second triangle which had an arcane focal point at each point and half way along each side. At all of these focal point stood a senior member of House Hector intoning their part of the ritual that was needed to power up the gate. The gate appeared to be fully charged and the family was just maintaining things until they were ready to open it.

Other than the guards, the only person to note our entrance was Hector himself. Looking up briefly, the vampire smiled then returned to reading through an intricate scroll.

According to the plan my job early on was to try and keep Hector talking since he appeared to like me for some reason. Susa said that she was going to try something and needed everyone focused on me and ignoring her for a bit. So plucking up my courage I interrupted Hector's study.

"Hector, who are we to be given to as tribute?" I asked, trying hard to keep my voice level: this close to the gate, my plan seemed a lot less solid.

"Oh, this is part of our ongoing treaty obligations with one of the trading companies out of The City of Brass," he said conversationally as he walked around the gate, making minor adjustments to the key foci. "Every 10 years we provide several exotic female slaves to our allies in token tribute as part of our ongoing trading relationship."

"Exotic?" I exclaimed, looking at everyone in the line; there was Storm, okay, I could see that one, and Susa. But the twins, Lia and me? We were pretty ordinary.

"Oh yes, high born virgin identical twins, a human warlock trained in her 'arts' by a succubus, a female Dark Elf... well, a female Dark Elf anything really falls into the exotic category; and your Elf friend, last of a noble line, turned thief. . ." he was talking, then Bam! He was right back in front of me lifting my head so that I was staring up into his eyes yet again. "And you," he said, cupping my face. "An accomplished warrior with a growing reputation, but who is also sexually a masochist."

Once again I felt the sudden pull of desire and heat, despite myself I let out a gasp of pure pleasure and felt my body heat up with desire as he moved his hand down from my face to my breasts, cupping one of them in his hand.

I felt my nipple harden at his touch as he leaned forward. "Truth be told, my pet," he whispered into my ear. "If we had found your Elf friend I was sorely tempted to keep you here for myself. It's been a century since I trained one such as you; I'd turn you, pet, into a true Blood Princess, one whose name would be feared through the very planes of existence."

His hand moved down, his fingers tracing lightly over my belly and down between my legs leaving trails of fire across my nerves. I moaned again, squirming slightly in my bonds as his fingers came to rest on my pussy. I stared up at him, and he looked down with a smile. He flicked his finger across my clitoris ring and I exploded in a climax, my body shuddering as I screamed with pleasure, my knees buckled and I pitched forward into Hector, my body limp and helpless. Somewhere in the back of my mind, I realized at that moment every eye in that garden was looking at me. Every woman wishing she was me, every man wanting to have me.

Except for Susa; who apparently had done what she needed to do, and took this time to finally speak up. "You know, Hector, these chokers are impressive and all, but you really needed to include a better locking mechanism."

And for some reason the sound of that choker, the one that had prevented her from using her magic, hitting the ground was loud enough to be heard clearly through the entire garden. The only other sound seemed to come from Susa's imp familiar who suddenly became visible and settled down on the warlock's left shoulder, laughing its perverted little head off.

Then all Nine Hells broke loose.

# Chapter Seven

With a sharp clear voice, Susa calmly spoke the most powerful spell she possessed. It was simply the vilest curse that I've ever heard: it drove through my ears, deep into my brain, and only stopped when it touched my soul, and I wasn't even the target. The after-effects of my orgasm were driven from my body and I pulled back out of Hectors grasp, my mind clear once again.

But Susa's spell had just hit every servant and Hector family member, including Hector himself, in the room with a curse so potent that it caused them physical harm.

The nearest family member's head exploded outright, showering the twins and Storm in blood and brains. Two other family members just died as their hearts stopped working. A few more fainted. The rest became ill and the smell of vomit mixed with the too-sweet smell of the flowers. Hector, believe it or not turned even paler.

And if that wasn't disturbing enough, wispy smoke appeared around the three corpses. Then as if blowing in the wind, all three pillars of smoke moved towards Susa who inhaled all three. This was what the patron of the covenant got out of the deal. The soul or spirit (or at least part of it) of every creature Susa killed with her magic became the patron's own. It did kick back some of the power into Susa though; and the warlock's eyes dilated wide as the pure soul energy flooded through her body.

But that was also just part of the distraction. From the shadows near the western entrance a slim throwing knife flew, shattering one of the fragile arcane conduits at the top of the gate: eldritch energy arced dangerously out of the gate as it became unstable; a single stream of power flicked out, finding one of the elite guards and cutting off one of his legs at the knee.

Following up her dagger throw, Lia herself ran out of the shadows. She dodged and wove her way through the still-stunned guards to end up next to me cutting my bonds.

At the same time Gwen entered the fight. My half-sister had seen better days; like Lia she was practically naked dressed only in a thong, her greased body covered with numerous cuts and abrasions. Apparently Lia had been right that Gwen could wriggle through the sewers, but only just.

Her dishevelled and almost completely naked appearance didn't seem to embarrass her at all as she stood proudly and raised her hands high. "Lightbringer!" she shouted. "Call forth your light to this dark place!"

With that a column of light crashed down into the garden centred on my half-sister. It exploded outwards, filling the garden with a light so bright that it almost had a physical force to it. Those who were aligned with House Hector and still standing after Susa's spell were thrown to the ground. This included Hector himself who was knocked back into one of his flower clumps.

As the light faded, Susa, myself, and my sisters were surrounded by a soft glowing light. I knew from previous fights that for a few minutes at least this light would reflect some of the more damaging blows we'd receive.

The Sun God's assistance had bought us time, and Lia was making use of it. "Here, take these," she said, as she pressed my weapons belt with my combat kopis and a pair of throwing knives into my hands. "Help me get to Susa with her coven blade, while Gwen keeps that vampire off balance."

Susa was currently surrounded by four guards, all of whom had recovered enough to clumsily try and stab her with their spears.

"Don't pick on the warlock," I shouted as I quickly belted on my knives and charged headlong into the four of them, drawing my blades as I went: I caught one guard completely flatfooted and clove through half his neck with my left hand kopis. Arterial blood sprayed, covering both me and one of the other guards in warm, bright red gore.

Another guard tried to use his spear to keep me at range, but I hooked the weapon with one blade and moved past its metal head. Before he realized what was happening, I swept the knife low, and cut the hamstrings on his right leg. Down the guard went, screaming bloody murder. That's the reason why I love the kopis; it might be short but the force it can deliver in a slash is like that of a weapon many times its length. The other two guards were still reeling from what had happened in the past fifteen seconds, so they just dropped their spears and ran as I came at them, leaving Lia free to help Susa.

And it was a good thing that I was able to give them that extra time. Like Gwen Lia hadn't had time to put on armour, she was wearing only a g-string, her weapon belt, and most importantly our bag of holding. She was busy helping Susa bind her weapons belt around her waist. It was clear that Susa's left hand wasn't working properly.

"What happened?" I asked over my shoulder, turning to meet a charge from two Hectorites who had drawn swords and attacked.

"Had to dislocate my thumb in order to get out of those bindings," said Susa, her voice hoarse, the tone I'd only ever heard her use in battle or after she'd just orgasmed. She pointed her coven dagger at one of the Hectorites charging at her and released a bolt of arcane energy striking him in the chest. The blast didn't kill him but he did stop his forward momentum.

"How did no one notice?"

"Well you and Hector were providing quite the distraction for the last part," replied Susa. "You've never screamed like that when we've fucked. I'm jealous."

"Not now, bitch," I snapped over my shoulder. "Alright, standard pairing. Susa, help Gwen and keep Hector off our backs. Lia, you're with me and we're going after the twins."

"Seriously?" asked Susa incredulously. She then screamed as she struck her left hand on the side of a wall reducing her dislocated digit.

"After all this shit, hells yes. The Asters are going to pay the balance of what they owe us, and then some," I replied. "Now go,"

"Oh, one last thing," said Lia as she quickly passed Susa and I pairs of panties. "I know we've all joked about armour of distraction but you two are taking it a little too far," said the Elf.

I was about to say something when I felt a lightning bolt pass a hair's breath away from my head. Looking up, I saw that the gate was become more unstable. I slipped my two kopis into their sheaths and then put on the g-string before heading towards the twins. This place was getting more unstable with every passing second.

Looking around, I saw that three guards and two Hectorites had herded both the twins and Storm into a corner and placed themselves before them. I could tell that they felt that their backs were protected and they only had to deal with threats coming from the front.

Obviously they've never fought an acrobat: Lia ran towards them once again, weaving back and forth and giving me a great view of her tight heart shaped ass clenching and unclenching as she moved (damn armour of distraction worked both ways) Seeing her go low, the guards lowered their spears to intercept her. Only at the last second Lia leaped up into the air past two of the guards slashing their arms as she flipped down into the centre of all five, their backs to her.

Crying out in pain, the two guards reflexively dropped

their spears. Before they could draw their short swords I was upon them: striking one guard in his wounded arm I cleaved it completely off with my right hand kopis. I used my left hand knife to parry a Hectorite attack. I was only partially successful, and I hissed in pain as the Hectorites sword left a gash on my left thigh.

Keeping their focus was just what Lia wanted me to do. Keeping out of the Hectorites' peripheral vision, Lia came up behind the Compact bastard that had wounded me and plunged her knives into either side of his neck, with a spray of arterial blood (which of course hit me) she wrenched the daggers free and kicked the body toward the other three guards.

"If you value your lives, get out of here now," I said in my most threatening voice. The power of the threat was increased by me being covered in blood and the fact that I had just dismembered someone in front of them; the Blood Princess had arrived.

One of the gate's arcane bolts struck the centre of one guard's scale-mailed chest; that might have helped. I mean, the bolt did disintegrate the metal links and the leather under-padding instantly, then burn through his chest down to the bone of his ribcage.

But I really feel it was my threatening tone and appearance that caused the two remaining guards to run for their lives and not look back.

That just left the twins, on their knees and covered in other people's blood and body parts, and Storm on the floor gasping for breath. The Dark Elf shuddered as arcane energy ran through her, small forks of lighting actually arcing between her ears and shoulders; the choker around her neck had tightened, blood dripping from its edges. Storm must have reflectively tried casting a spell.

"Ah hells," I cursed. "Gwen would never let this one rest if I didn't." I reached down and unfastened the collar from Storm's neck. For the moment Storm just lay there gasping, and drawing in deep breaths like it was the greatest thing ever. Reaching down, I grabbed the twins under their arms and pulled them up. "We're getting the both of you out of here. Your family owes us a lot of gold, and I'm planning on collecting," I told them as I cut through the rope binding their hands.

"Annie," Storm coughed struggling to rise to her feet, "I know the house's layout: free my hands and we stand a much better chance of all of us getting out of here."

"Turn around," I said. As she complied, I brought one kopis down on the bonds and chopped through them with one stroke.

Now that her hands were free, Storm turned to me, smiling a big old friendly smile.

Before she could say a word, I slugged her in the jaw. "*That* was for the needles, bitch!" I snapped. "Now, what's the shortest way to the east exit?"

Her smile turned to a look of pure venom, but Storm kept things in perspective, and pointed towards one of the gates.

"Stop them, kill some of them if you have to, but *stop them!*" I heard Hector scream in growing frustration. Strangely, Hector's voice did not affect me as he had before. It may have been because I was in a fight, which was where I was at my strongest, it may have been because Hector was preoccupied with trying to keep the gate from exploding, or maybe that Hector was just too angry with the situation to sound charming. Whatever it was, the vampire now just sounded like a tired old man.

His two plate mailed guards, however, were anything but tired. They moved with a startling speed towards where I stood with the twins and Storm. As they closed, one of them caught another arcane bolt from the gate, I gulped seeing that the bodyguard was staggered but continued moving forward.

I then heard Susa laugh with a note of irony, "It's the

metal; all that armour is attracting the gate's discharges. Being naked is keeping us safe. Now let's see how they react to thunder!" She let out an ear-splitting scream, triggering a spell that caught both bodyguards and hurled them hard against the nearby wall.

"Well, here's to being naked," I said as I charged the bodyguards just as they were trying to get up from the ground.

Grabbing one of their helmets, I wrenched it off with the idea of ramming a kopis between his eyes. Only as I looked down I saw that the guard was already dead, or rather undead. Its partially decomposed skin was stretched thinly over its skull. The creature's gums had long since receded, making its teeth looked like long daggers ready to tear through flesh. Its eyes glowed a sickly green colour. With an inhuman cry it backhanded me away before I could recover from the shock. Gwen's magical light flared, absorbing much of the blow and I was able to roll with the rest. However, the creatures touch was chilling, causing me to break out in goose bumps despite the warmth of the evening.

"They're Wights of some sort. Careful you don't want them to touch you. They're life drainers," shouted Susa in warning. The backlash of her magic was more evident on her naked body than usual. Her breasts, stomach and back were covered in thin welts. The fingers on her right hand were burnt; the skin around her right eye was blue and yellow with bruising, and her left eye full of blood.

"Ah Gwen, we've got undead here!" I shouted at my sister. I've no problem facing off against undead when I have to, but clerics of the Sun God are particularly adept at handling such creatures.

"Back to the shadows that spawned you! Bother this place no more!" shouted Gwen in a commanding voice.

Both undead warriors staggered and erupted in flames of bright white as Gwen's invocation caused them to retreat once again. The one without a helmet screamed and held its head in its hands as black smoke poured from its nose and ears. Not wanting to miss the opportunity to strike while someone's down, Lia let fly with one of her narrow throwing knives. It lanced deep into the creatures open mouth of the helmetless Wight. The Wight twitched once, then fell to the ground, once again dead.

I charged forward and slashed hard against the remaining Wight. Unfortunately, I only managed to dent the plate armour. The Wight swung the butt end its spear, slamming it hard into my wounded thigh. Along with the pain, I once again I felt the goose bumps as cold spread throughout my body, locking my legs in place.

Seeing that I was unable to move, the Wight reversed his spear and thrust it at a point between my bare breasts. I blocked the blow with my crisscrossed kopis, just an inch before my breast bone. But in concentrating on me, the Wight left itself open to attacks from my teammates. Once again Lia rolled behind the creature, her daggers flashing out. One slid off the metal breastplate, but the other bit deep into the leather covered armpit. A bolt of fiery energy struck the head of the creature, and the helmet glowed red-hot. A bolt of lightning slammed into the side of the Wight as Storm joined the fight on our side this time.

As all this was happening, I suddenly felt a surge of hope and confidence, as the healing powers of the Lightbringer's grace infused me with new vigour and allowed me to move again; Gwen had asked her God to heal me from the injuries I'd so far incurred.

My strength renewed, I backhanded my left kopis down hard upon the Wight's glowing helmet. The softened metal buckled under the strike, and I heard a sizzling sound as the still-hot metal struck flesh. The undead creature shook once and then dropped its spear in a vain attempt to remove its glowing red helmet from its head.

It didn't have a chance to finish the action as it fell

under the effects of Susa, Storm and Gwen's magical attacks.

The few remaining guards had rallied and blocked the entrance. Right, one last fight and we were free of this place. "Gwen, see to the twins," I said, starting to march hard towards the remaining guards. "Susa, Lia, Storm, we're going to punch a hole through those guards and get the Hells out of here."

"*ENOUGH!*" Hector shouted, and everything just stopped, everyone frozen in place. The gate did not seem to be any more stable than before, but my guess was that if he lost us the stable gate was meaningless. "You ladies will drop your weapons now and surrender or I will string you up by your tits until they rip off your chests," he commanded.

No one seemed ready to drop their weapons. In fact, Gwen and Lia seemed ready to strike against the Vampire, while Susa glanced at Storm and motioned towards the cluster of guards.

The sound of my fighting knives hitting the floor seemed to surprise everyone but Hector. "Well at least the Blood Princess showed some sense; what about the rest of you?" he asked, turning his attention away from me and towards the others.

Which is just what I wanted him to do: I flipped the Wight's solid metal spear up with my foot and caught it in my now empty hands. Hector did see me, but too late: I was already running with my full weight behind the strike; he turned to face me just as I struck, driving the spear's head into his body, through his heart, and out the other side.

The attack hurt Hector, I could see that from the expression on his face, but all he did was laugh at me. "You stupid bitch!" he said with a scathing laugh. "Shoving a metal stake through a vampire's heart doesn't stop him," he backhanded me across the face, knocking me back towards the twins and Storm. "It just makes them *pissed off.*"

I looked up at him from where I fell with a shit eating grin. "Really? Well, that's two things I learned tonight then," I said.

"Oh? And what was the other thing you learned?" he mockingly asked.

"That metal channels lightening really well," I said, pointing to the gate behind him.

Hector face turned grey for a second as he realized the implications of what I just said. He grabbed at the front of the spear to pull it out, but he was too late: a bolt of arcane energy arced out from the gate and hit the metal spear. Energy flashed down the shaft and punched a fist size hole through the leader of the House. The vampire screamed as energy burst through his body, turning him instantly into a pile of smoking ash.

I reached down, got my kopis, and stood up again as everyone looked at me and where Hector had been in complete silence. "Well, come on, let's move," I said, kicking the twins into motion, and then pushing them towards the exit. The guards, seeing that their master was now dead, parted and wisely let us through. Quickly, Susa, Gwen, Lia and Storm followed.

# Chapter Eight

The news of Hector's death spread quickly throughout the house. The guards decided that it made more sense to let us go instead of dying in a pointless attempt at revenge. Once outside House Hector's estate, we all piled into Gwen's cart and headed towards the nearest Sun God's mission.

Once there Gwen officially granted us sanctuary. Believe it or not, Compact or House authorities cannot cross onto holy ground in the pursuit of any fugitives; it's actually part of the Compact. I guess it was the price the city paid to the Gods for the trade routes to the God Sea.

After we saw to our wounds but before we contacted our backstabbing son of a bitch employers, Susa and I had some more pressing business to attend to. Legally we were still House Hector's property, and anyone in the City of Gates could turn us in for a nice bounty. A quick check by Gwen indicated that our initial impression was correct. The brands could not be magically healed like a normal burn scar, altered apparently but not fully removed. Fortunately, Compact Law gave us another alternative, one which the Church of the Lightbearer always has available. Under Compact Law, a person's status as either free or slave could be clarified if on the limb that bore the brand a tattoo of a broken chain was added. So the first couple of hours of sanctuary were spent getting inked by a cleric of the church. He did a surprisingly good tattoo around my mid-thigh, and I asked if he did commission work. He laughed and politely said no. Storm, bless her paranoid Dark Elf heart, had me go first and insisted that the cleric use the same needle on her that he had used on me.

Once we were legally free, we met with the Asters. Who, for some unknown reason, were surprised to hear from us. When the twins were returned, the Asters paid the balance of what they owed us. They then paid us a bonus equal to our original fee to keep quiet regarding their breach of our contract. Selling kin into slavery is one thing, but breaching *any* contract is a really big no-no. Within Compact society your commitments to contracts is your only true worth. Susa and I both decided to keep our jewelled navel rings but Lia fenced the remainder of the jewellery Hector had adorned us with prior to our presentation. Once it was liquefied into hard cash and combined with what Aster had paid us it was easily the best haul that the Black Bitches had ever managed.

We blew through most of it in about two months. To start, Gwen guilted us into a large donation to her church in thanks for the sanctuary. We would have donated something, but trust me, Gwen can really guilt people. Susa then located a place that sold those magical high heeled boots and she, Lia and I picked up a pair. Okay, we all picked up two pairs, but I really couldn't decide between the black and red leather.

I was surprised to hear from Gwen that Storm also made quite a large donation to the church herself. Overall, I think the Dark Elf and my team have reached an understanding. We stay out of her way and she stays out of ours. How long that will last is your guess, personally I give it six months before she and Susa crossed spells again.

Two weeks after the rescue, house Aster was rocked again by the twins' disappearance. A month searching the city had proved fruitless and so Aster had the twins officially declared dead.

The funeral was a brilliant affair, the social event of the month. The Black Bitches were of course not invited to the funeral. Even if we were we would not have gone; we had a previous engagement at the Dark Queen; the City of

Gates' largest and best brothel; they had a popular new pair of 'performers.' These identical twins had invited us to a private party at the brothel which Lia, Susa and I (Gwen politely indicated that she had church duties that night) greatly enjoyed. Everyone awakened the next afternoon sore, but that was fine. We had completed another job recently where we had been paid with two sets of expensive body jewellery so we were in no great need of funds.

House Hector did not last the month after its namesake's death. With the Hectors in breach of their treaties, the other Houses pounced. First the lapsed treaties were taken over. Then a physical attack was made upon the estate. In order to survive, what remained of the Hectorites leadership broke up the remaining assets and got themselves adopted into other Houses. Three weeks after Hector was destroyed by my hand, it was as if the House never existed.

So now I know how the world (or the Gates at least) really works. All of the Compact families have to be led by creatures at least a powerful as an elder vampire. If they weren't then Hector would have ruled over the Gates years (decades? centuries?) ago. Does that mean that mortals such as myself are just pawns in a games that is so old it can never really be understood?

Thoughts for another day. Right now I have bigger problems: I can't sleep at night. Well, I can sleep, but my dreams are so real and vivid that I wake up screaming. They all centre on Hector. Some are incredibly erotic and I awake screaming in pleasure, others are downright terrifying. They all end with me being grabbed by someone and woken up, or ending up near the front of Hector's old estates. If I sleep during the day, I'm fine. If I share a bed with someone I'm fine. But at night; alone; not good.

This has led me to believe that Hector isn't dead. Both Gwen and Susa have told me that vampires can have phylacteries, so just because he was turned to dust by a lightning bolt doesn't mean that he won't be back some day. And he still has an interest in me.

    Shit.

# Knife Work: The Blood Princess Saga Book 2

# Acknowledgements

When you start writing one of the first things you discover is that while many might say they want to help with reading through a first draft or proof reading, those who actually do so are few and far between.

To both Matts; who, despite being just as busy as everyone else, actually did read the story and gave useable feedback. An extra special shout out to Matt O who once again took on the role of copy editor. Hopefully it was easier this time than the first.

To Anson: for allowing me to use the image he created as my cover. If you like his work then I'd suggest taking a look at this other pieces at http://anson7.deviantart.com.

# Chapter One

I hate the slave pens.

For anyone who's grown up in The City of Gates, the pens are always the great fear.

One little mistake; walk down the wrong alleyway at the wrong time; miss one repayment on a debt. Or your family ends up on the losing end of one of the countless Compact tit-for-tat fights. And you end up on that podium stripped naked; your features crudely brought to the attention of the buyers, by some snake. Often literally snakes; the Nagas were heavily involved in the slave trade both in the city and through the gates.

Despite the humiliation of being sold to someone you may know, people from the Gates consider ourselves lucky if we're sold in the city. Any slave taken through one of the gates never comes back. Stories abounded about what the fates of these slaves are. Everything from toiling in deep elemental salt mines (why it's always salt mines I have no idea), made into sex toys for formless blobs, having their souls ripped from their bodies and made into currency, and perhaps the worst to my mind, sold as food.

These feelings of fear were increased for me now that I wore a slave brand on my right ass cheek. A permanent reminder to just how thin the thread between freedom and slavery is in the Gates.

Strangely the brand has added to the legend of the Blood Princess. One story has me as a freed gladiator trying to earn enough money to buy my brother/twin sister/pet wolf from the Compact family that's currently holding them over me. In another I'm really a barbarian princess whose tribe has been enslaved after a valiant but fruitless war with some unknown empire. After months of being used as a sex slave, I escaped to the City of Gates and had become a sell sword to gather an army to regain my homelands. The most bizarre story I've heard is that I'm some sort of slave/assassin out to avenge my owner's honour from the Compact Family that destroyed them. The really strange thing all these stories seemed to share is the idea that I always had the brand, as opposed to getting it less than three months ago.

The total effect of all these stories had been increased exposure for the Black Bitches. Which isn't necessary a good thing. Many potential employers are looking for some discretion in their endeavours, something that a group with a public reputation, can't easily offer. This meant that we had to adjust to a new kind of clientele, and a new kind of job.

The bodyguard work for House Merath was an excellent example of the new kind of jobs we're getting. The minor Compact family trade house wanted us to bodyguard someone for a couple of days. Hiring bodyguards outside the normal family circle was seen as a status symbol for the person being hired for (I'm so important that my own 'loyal' retainers might kill me).

Arriving at the estate, I was met by the house chamberlain who ushered me into the home and then to a meeting with the house matron. As we walked, I got a feeling of disdain from the chamberlain. House Merath was conservative and surprisingly religious for a Compact family. They supposedly held The Builder of Cities in high regard.

So the distain was not surprising given that I walked in my usual metal reinforced black leather body thong, blood red bracers and greaves and more knifes than a Compact house kitchen. In short, I stood out. This is what you want at least part of your bodyguard detail to do, though. One of the bodyguard's jobs in a public setting is intimidation. It's the 'try and fuck with my charges and I'll fuck you up first' idea. Orcs, Trolls, and Minotaurs can do this based on size alone. I'm much shorter than those races so I have to rely on my street rep to keep things quiet. This is why I dress so brashly as the Blood Princess. People need to know that someone is dangerous and that there is going to be a price to pay if you cross them.

When we entered the room, the matron was already standing to meet us. Surprisingly she had greying hair and looked old (well, older). Magic being able to do what it does, it's a rare Compact member that doesn't spend money to keep looking like they're in their 20s (or younger). Yet, despite her appearing in her 50s, the matron wasn't completely anti magic. Her gravity defying breasts and slim figure certainly had a magical 'helping hand'. Not to mention the cool look that she gave me which seemed to lower the temperature in the room to where I shivered. Or that the only name/title I was allowed to use to refer to her was 'Her Ladyship'. With a welcome like this, I started to wonder how the Black Bitches got this job in the first place.

However, the house matron did not allow personal preference to get in the way of her how she conducted business. She explained that her great granddaughter was just coming of age, and as part of a growing responsibility in the house she was given the task of purchasing several new slaves or the houses farms.

The great granddaughter, whose name was Lexi, was described to me as a proper young Compact lady, who was a bit sheltered. The slave purchase was meant to expose her to some of the harsher parts of life as a step towards her becoming more involved in the houses economic and business affairs. The Bitches and I were supposed to keep her safe and not let any lesson from becoming too overwhelming. But if some street safety lessons were needed to be instilled then that was fine as well.

Only thing was, like most Compact brats, Lexi was plenty worldly already.

Human and barely 18, Lexi had the best figure magic could alter, and she wanted others to know it. As soon as we left the compound, with two personal servants and a house accountant, she'd shorn the conservative dress she had been wearing while with the Matron, and handed it to her servant. Underneath she was wearing a brief bikini which she added a sheer hip scarf decorated with dozens of bangles that clanked together as loudly as Gwen's chainmail. The sensible silk and leather slippers were replace by a pair of fuck me pumps, and she added a wide leather belt with an overseer's rod, to complete the look. Finally with a couple of command words the latest in magically animated tattoos appeared on her upper left arm and lower back, and bright attention seeking makeup appeared on her face.

The servants, who were already in similar though less expensive ensembles, cooed in approval. The accountant gave an impression of disapproval but he seemed to have forgotten the Lexi had a head because his eyes never rose above her chest.

I just looked heavenward and wondered which of our gods had decided to test my patience.

# Chapter Two

"Now *this* is more appropriate attire for someone being guarded by the Blood Princess," said Lexi as she neared the waiting carriage. One thing was clear as Compact girl walked; she knew how to work those pumps. That caused me even more dread. This was obviously Lexi's normal attire. And that meant that she was far more used to the loose moral lifestyle of the normal Compact Brat than the conservative notions that Marath publicly adhered to.

Once at the carriage I looked around and seeing nothing unusual, loaded up my charge and her entourage. After one last glance around, I gave an all clear signal to the driver and carriage guard and settled in myself. Once we were going I kept an eye on the sidewalks, adopting the air of professional detachment that is a sign of a good bodyguard.

"It was my idea to hire you," said Lexi all of a sudden.

I glanced over to her long enough so that she knew that I heard her.

"I hear things about you, Princess, things I'd like to find out if they're true or not; and I always get what I want," she said with a somewhat husky voice which sent the servants into a fit of dirty giggles and the accountant to fix his gaze permanently outside pretending not to hear anything.

"Perhaps after we return from the purchase today Miss, but not before," I replied. Hey possible was better than an outright no in this circumstance.

Lexi took that riposte at face value. For several minutes she seemed satisfied, then glancing down at my freed slave tattoo around my leg, she asked, trying to sound seductive. "Why would anyone let you go?"

"He didn't have a choice," I said in a matter of fact tone.

"Oh? Why did your master not have a choice?" she asked trying to the play evil seductress.

"I drove an 8 foot metal spear through his heart. Then a lightning bolt hit the spear and turned him to ash," I replied with a perfectly straight face. "Hard to object when you're ash."

That caught the little bitch flat footed. She hadn't expected me to have such a violent answer given with no emotion. That I treated killing my 'master' with such a trivial manner and still lived stopped her talking for the rest of the trip. Once we arrived at the pens, though, Lexi seemed to have recovered from the shock. I got out of the carriage first, and while I was looking for threats outside the little bitch grabbed and squeezed my ass as she came by.

As the Compact brat strolled off giggling with her cohorts I was now regretting not bringing Susa with me on this job. The warlock loved nothing better than teaching wannabe Compact kids some lessons on how the world *really* worked. But I hadn't. At the time I thought that things would go smoother without Susa being around *because* she loved teaching wannabe Compact kids some lessons on how the world *really* worked; which usually included a sexual encounter that even a jaded Compacter would never forget. I'll not make that mistake twice. Next time Susa comes along, and I'll risk the scars and scandal that might result.

I did have Lia our elven thief and scout with me though. As per our plan, Lia was somewhere out in the shadows of the city watching my back.

This brings me back to hating the slave pens, as I kept one eye on my client's hands and the other on the crowd.

Fortunately, most of the thieves with the city know me by reputation and know that as long as they don't bother my client I won't bother them. Important lesson that; you just have to look aware and competent; thieves like easy marks. So not looking like low hanging fruit is usually all that you need. It also helps just a bit that Lia had let the thieves' guild know about our willingness to have the live and let live attitude guide our actions.

For me that meant that the only real threat to Lexi (other than the usual Gate craziness) was from body snatchers. With Lexi being from a Compact family, even a minor one, she was definitely a target for either some off world slaver (they always pay more for noble slaves) or local kidnap gang (who know that Compact families are often willing to pay a significant ransom to get their loved ones back). That's what Lia's real job was: follow anyone who was following us, and let me know of the threat. If and when the threat attacked she'd ambush them in return.

Lexi appeared to know where to go because she headed straight to the Slaver's Guild headquarters. Someone must have been expecting her. She hadn't come within 100 feet of the place before three well-dressed slave brokers came running up to her.

"Mistress Merath. Mistress Merath. Thank you for gracing us with your presence today," said the three of them almost en sync.

Lexi took a teenager's pleasure in having adults kowtow to her. Beaming, she replied "Thank you all, a pleasure to meet you all again. However, I did not come here today for such pleasantries, but rather on business. So let us take a look at your offerings today."

Ah, the arrogance of the Compact. Lexi had just demanded to cherry-pick the slaver's best. If someone outside of the Compact had just demanded to do what Lexi had, she'd be in danger of ending up on the slave block that day. But Lexi *was* Compact, so the slaver's response was "Of course Mistress, right this way."

Entering the actual slave kennels was where the fun really started. Lexi could walk on level ground in those pumps of hers, but the broken ground of the pens caused her no end of problems.

After she nearly tripped into a puddle of human sewage, I suggested that for the purposes of dignity she might want to change back into her slippers while in the pens.

For a briefest of seconds, a look of confusion went across Lexi's face, but then she said, "I believe your suggestion is quite a valid one, Annie." A look of self-deprecation came across her face as she continued, "I appear to be having a bad shoe day."

I smiled at the genuine humility. That little piece of humanity made me realize that there might be more to her than what I first suspected.

As the attendant with her other clothes came up with the shoes, I heard her ask, "Lexi, you've never had problems walking in these shoes before, what's wrong?"

"Nervous about the sales I guess," then looking directly at the attendant she said "Don't worry about it."

The attendant dropped the subject without further mention.

Changing her shoes appeared to have an unusual effect upon Lexi. Despite her inexperience with how the slave pens worked; she walked with a new air of confidence. She pulled out her overseer rod and moved between the various slaves as if knowing what she was actually looking for. Lexi by-passed most of the younger men and women, giving no more than cursory glance to the eye candy of either sex.

I started to become even more impressed with her, as I saw a pattern emerge to what she was doing. In men she looked for older males who were still in reasonable shape.

Lexi would then ask if they had children and if the mothers of those children were here. In the case of women she looked for good birthing hips or mothers with children. She actually took the time and reformed several families and bought all of them together. In one case, she actually bought up three generations of a family in one shot.

She ended up talking to all of the brokers at one point or another, but she did so in a respectful manner, and she strove to make good deals without leaving hard feelings.

The accountant was at first nonplused about the money being spent but after one particular sale he said, "Mistress Mareth, you seem to be loading us up on many slaves that will only have a short work life?"

Lexi just cut him off. "Slave families are a far better long term investment. Older men are less hot headed and prone to escape attempts. They'll work hard cause they know that's the only thing that keeps their families together. Not to mention that they have proof of virility. The women have all survived child birth at least once, which mean their chance of surviving another is higher. They've also produced children who have survived into early childhood, so they produce healthy stock. Give another five years of such family purchases and our farm slaves will be self-sustaining."

The accountant looked at her impressed and he actually bowed to her. "You have your father's good sense," he said.

"My mother's actually; she was a Hector and they all have a good head for business," was her reply.

The accountant just bowed again and seemed embarrassed that he made such an oversight.

"That was strange," said Lexi's other attendant, who looked bored but was still attentive.

"What was?" I asked.

"Lexi hates her mother; she's a real daddy's girl. That's the first time in 3 years that I have ever heard her say a nice thing about her mother," the attendant replied.

"Well, things can change," I said sagely. Here I was only a year older and it sounded like I knew the world.

But as the day progressed, Lexi's dealings not only got good deals but the respect of the entire slave pens as well. Brokers started to compete for her business, overseers to search for slaves they thought she would like.

By the end of the day, she was holding court in a corner of the pens furthest away from the stench. An awning had been erected for shade and a comfortable high backed chair with side table had been brought out for my mistress to sit at. Petitioners were coming to her to offer their slaves just so they could say that she had deemed them worthy to purchase from.

Finally Lexi announced that she was done for the day. Turning to the accountant she said. "See to the details of the purchases, I believe that the grand dam gave you signing authority?"

"Yes Mistress," replied the accountant giving my charge the respect that she was due.

"Good. Exercise it," she said in a note of dismissal.

Lexi then stretched showing off her fine figure to everyone around. She then turned and smiled ruefully directly at me. I liked that smile and I liked that Lexi was giving me some attention. I mentally kicked myself for my hesitancy of the morning and wished I'd taken Lexi up on her offer.

"Now that I'm done with the business of the day, I'm interested in some more personal matters," she gave me a flirtatious smile and said "What sort of sex slaves do you have?" she asked the overseers.

A sudden flash of jealousy hit me. We had all but agreed to hook up and now she was going to pick up some half trained slut instead?

The brokers didn't seem to care. They all but bolted away and headed out to grab what they thought were their best sluts.

The first two came back with pretty standard fare. In all honesty the sex slave market in the City of Gates is pretty slim. The standard thinking of the overseers seems to be that any girl (or boy to be fair) who's pretty, and whose will has been so broken that they'll let anyone do whatever to them passively, is all that it takes to make a good sex slave. Want something more lively? Just dose them with dragon piss or some other aphrodisiac and let the party begin.

That's what they offered Lexi early on; pretty and broken, with no spirit left to them whatsoever. Poor choices for Lexi who deserved someone more lively. She saw this and glanced over to me as if to ask my opinion on the matter. Pleased that Lexi would value my opinion, I would shake my head and frown at the poor girls that they had chosen.

The last broker came forward, and I was a little more hopeful for this one. He's was one of the first to cotton to the fact my Lexi actually knew what she was doing when it came to slaves and had adjusted his approach appropriately.

The bed warmer he brought forward was draped in a cloak with the cowl up so that all features of the slave were hidden.

"Ah, Mistress Lexi, I bring before you a true mystery. Found wandering the streets a month ago. Naked, with no memory of her past. Branded but with a mark not used by any house in the city. Fluent in our language but with an accent no one has ever heard before. She was taken to the City Watch and placed into their lost and found kennels. As per city law since no one claimed her I was contacted and received the contract from the city to sell her on the market," started the broker clearly relishing the story.

Mysterious slave? No memory? At least this guy knew how to build anticipation.

"May I present Ricci," said the broker. With a flourish of a true story teller, he flung off the slave's hood.

It revealed a human female, still in her late teens, with long silver hair, silver eyes, pale complexion, and fine symmetrical features.

The expression that those features wore was one of confusion at first, then that changed to a quick assessment as she glanced around. Once her eyes landed on Lexi, the expression changed. She was checking Lexi out as hard as Lexi was checking her out. When Lexi glanced at me the girl caught the gesture and looked at me as well. Both girls shared the same expression "Well?" it asked.

I nodded slightly; this was more like it, something worthy of her. Lexi appeared to agree, and indicated to the broker that he should continue.

Of course next was the big reveal, with the broker grabbing the top of the cloak and ripping it off showing the body of the naked girl underneath.

On looking at her, I was both turned on and repulsed. The girl had had some major magical adjustments done to her, but the result of those adjustments caused almost everyone to stare; and caused me to inwardly groan.

Her appearance had been clearly altered by a male. It was like running down a check list to see if she had all the proper 'features' that past for the current male definition of female beauty.

Long hair of any colour that's not brown. Check.

Big expressive eyes any colour that's not brown. Check.

Athletic build. Check.

Petite frame. Check.

Slim waist. Check.

Tight heart shaped ass. Check.

Modify the lower leg's tendons so that the slave could only walk on the balls of her feet, thus eliminating the need for heels to give better definition to the slave's legs and ass. Check

Perky C cup breasts. Check. (Why do men always talk about cup size when it comes to women's breasts. Like they'd actually know the difference between a B and C cup if they were shown the two.)

The lean frame coupled with large breasts and a well formed ass of course perpetuated the idea that the perfect woman was a Half-Elf and making it nearly impossible for us pure blood races to match that ideal without magical assistance.

At least they kept her pussy intact and didn't enlarge the clitoris or replace it with a penis.

On top of those physical changes they added the usual current fashion trends: no body hair, body piercings and half a dozen small tattoos around the body (including of course the almost mandatory tramp stamp on the lower back).

About the only real modification that was off the check list was what had been done to her left arm. There a half sleeve tattoo had been inked that looked like some of the spell effects I'd seen surrounding Susa's limbs as she got ready to fire off a really potent spell. Ricci also wore a slave bracelet on that wrist that at first appeared to be integrated into design but looking closer I realized that the bracelets links were actually embedded into the skin.

As she turned to show off her back I did a double take when I saw the brand burnt into her right ass cheek. It was the same brand that Susa and I came up with after we escaped from House Hector. As far as we knew no one used that brand, yet it was on a third person clear as day. I tried my best to keep my features even but I didn't succeed. But no matter Ricci had captured everyone's attention.

"Does this meant with your expectations, mistress?" the broker asked Lexi.

"Yes, this is much closer to what I was looking for," replied Lexi. "Do you have an examination room where I could more closely inspect the slave?"

"Of course, right over there," said the broker gesturing toward a series of small buildings. He gestured to one of the overseers who collared and leashed Ricci. The broker then was handed the leash and made to follow Lexi.

"I believe that all that I require is my bodyguard," said my mistress tartly to the broker. She took the leash from the broker's hand and headed towards one of the buildings.

Since I had been included, I turned and followed the two hot teens.

# Chapter Three

The 'examination' space was a smallish room that was magically bright as day inside even though there were no windows and only one door. Built more for privacy than comfort, the room was designed to allow privileged purchasers to make sure that slaves performed as the slaver claimed.

There were several lounges built along one side of the building where the potential buyer could sit with a degree of comfort. The remainder of the area was open for slave display. Off to one side was a saw horse that a slave could be bent over and tied down, allowing the slave's assets to be examined in greater detail if required. In the centre was a raised dais which rotated to allow a buyer 360' view. Manacles which also rotated were available to keep the slave in the appropriate posture.

"Chain her to the dais, hands above her head, legs spread to match her shoulders and with her toes barely touching the floor," instructed Lexi as we entered the room. She then sauntered over to one of the lounges and sat down.

I did as instructed, but with mixed feelings. Overwhelmingly I wanted to please my mistress and was happy to follow through with her request. But in the back of my mind a part of me was disturbed. I hated the slave pens, I hated slavery, and here I was leaping to help to sell another girl into sexual slavery.

But the slave would be so lucky to be owned by my mistress so really it was only helping her, the louder voice said drowning out my concerns.

When I was done chaining Ricci onto the dais, I stepped back and started its rotation. The fear/thrill/humiliation of such an exposed display had started to have an effect upon the slave. Her pussy lips were swollen, her nipples were rock hard and her eyes were dilated. The room was hot enough to cover her with sweat, but she was breathing hard as the flight or fight response to danger kicked in. She looked down to where Lexi sat in the shadows waiting to hear her fate. Turning her head to keep my mistress in site as the dais slowly rotated.

To my surprised I was almost as aroused as Ricci was and stood there struggling to remain still, awaiting my mistress's next command.

"Annie you look so hot, strip off that armour and your weapons so that you're more comfortable," said Lexi

"Thank you mistress, it is quite warm in here," I said. We were safe in this room so what was the danger? I quickly removed my weapons and then stripped out of my studded leather body thong and hung them all on several pegs along one side of the wall. Below them I place my reinforced leather boots. Now only dressed in my silk g-string I started to move back next to Ricci in the middle of the room.

"Did I tell you to stop Annie?" said Lexi, with a note of annoyance.

I turned to look at Lexi and realized with much embarrassment that I have failed to follow my mistress's instructions. Quickly I slipped out of the offending panties.

"Such disregard of my instructions will not be tolerated, Annie. It sets a bad example to Ricci as to how I expect my instructions to be carried out. Go over to the sawhorse, bend over it, spread your legs, and grab your ankles," my mistress commanded.

I quickly moved towards the bar.

"On the balls of your feet Annie, I shouldn't have to tell you that as well," said Lexi annoyed.

Keeping my heels off the ground, I did as I was commanded. Soon I was watching the rest of the room with my head between my legs. The dais had stopped so that Ricci was now staring directly at me while Lexi was moving my direction.

My mistress had removed her top and wrap and was now only dressed in her panties. In her hand was the overseer rod that she had brought with her.

"I believe 5 strokes will suffice for you to remember," she said as she laid the first stroke with the rod across my raised ass.

"Thank you mistress, for helping me remember," I said in a calm voice. While the stroke hurt, it was nothing compared to what Brutal even started with me now a days. If anything the stimulation caused me to become even more aroused.

If Lexi seemed to be disturbed by my lack of reaction my mistress did not show it. She just gave me the next stroke, and I replied the same, only this time I couldn't keep the arousal from my voice.

And so it went for the five strokes. By the fifth stroke I was having difficulty keeping in place, I wanted to writhe in the pleasure that the pain was giving me.

After she was done, Lexi turned to Ricci "I hope you understand my expectations if I choose to buy you slave?"

"Yes mistress," replied Ricci automatically.

"Good. Now that that unpleasantness has been dealt with, Annie you can let go of your ankles and stand again," she said to me.

I did so, remembering this time to keep on the balls of my feet.

"Annie, I understand that you excel at knife play."

"I have been taught the basics, Mistress, but have really only used them on two people," I replied. Knife play was the only dominant side of pain work that I'd actually practised, and that had come about more by accident than anything. Brutal had introduced it to me as part of me exploring the relationship between pain and sex, and it represents his one and only failure to this point.

Brutal is all about the "illusion" of danger in his pain work. He wants you to think you're in danger, which speeds the whole pain leads to sexual arousal which leads you to be able to take more pain loop. As long as a part of your brain knows the danger is not really real it allows you to surrender more to the stimulation.

My only problem resulted from the simple fact that I am one of the best knife fighters in the city. And when Brutal approached me all dangerous and threatened me with a knife his technique and body language was so bad that any illusion of danger was shattered and all I could do was laugh. This caused such a hurt expression on his face that I ended up laughing even harder.

"What," he asked true anger rising in his voice.

"Bracken," I said invoking the safeword which ended the session.

"I'm sorry Brutal, but your approach with that knife, your body language and the knife itself…it's all just…so bad," I said I still couldn't keep the amusement out of my voice.

This stung Brutal pretty hard. The last thing, a top wants to hear from his bottom when setting up a story is laughter.

"But you're still tied up, I still have you completely under my control?" he countered.

I looked at him strangely and for the first time I realized that while it was no one's fault, there had been a fundamental misunderstanding between Brutal and myself as far as the level of illusion there had been. He had me tied spread eagle to a wood frame which would have held most people. Problem was I wasn't most people. Gripping the top of the frame I used my whole body to twist the furniture stressing the joints. Then I pulled down on the joint with one of my hands and pressed up with the other. With a sharp crack the frame broke and I was not only able to free my hands but had a jagged piece of wood in each hand to use as a weapon.

"You've never really put me into a situation where I was truly in peril, I could always get out. I just thought that was supposed be part of the illusion so I never questioned it until now. Did you think that I was always helpless in our sessions?

I swear I could have told him his dick was small and he would have been less humiliated.

He didn't say a word; he just put down the knife and left the dungeon. Now to his credit he returned within five minutes and simply asked "alright how do you look intimidating with a knife?"

This led to a series of sessions over the next few weeks; where I showed him how to wield a knife and he taught me knife play as a sexual act.

It was those skills that Lexi asked me to employ now.

"That's not what I've seen, Annie, you're quite good. I want to see how Ricci reacts," my mistress commanded.

"Yes, mistress," I replied simply, I went over to where my weapons were and took up one of my throwing knives. It was a short, narrow-bladed weapon, perfectly balanced and of course razor sharp.

"No, not that one I want you to use one of your kopis," said Lexi.

I paused. The kopis were fighting knives. Eighteen inches of concave steel, they invoked words like brutal and deadly, not finesse or elegant which is usually what you want in a knifeplay implement.

However, mistress had wanted me to use the kopis and I'd already displeased her once so I put back the throwing knife and took up the fighting blade.

Seeing that I was complying, Lexi once again took her place on the shadow hidden lounge.

Stepping up to Ricci, I followed the script of Brutal's story faithfully. Ricci saw me coming with the knife and I saw fear and anticipation in her eyes, but not outright terror: Exactly where I wanted her emotionally. I proceeded to explore her body with the kopis scraping along the edge of the blade across her body, listening to her breath, watching her reactions, and feeling the reactions of her body as she involuntarily twitched under the edge. Always there was the potential of being cut, of drawing blood, with knife play and it was from the danger that the arousal arose.

I did all of this with confidence and concentration as you'd expect from one skilled with knives. But there was no arousal on my part. Causing pleasure in someone else implied too much commitment upon my part to take pleasure in that act myself.

This did not mean that I was not having the desired effect upon Ricci. By the time I had found her erogenous zones and started to concentrate upon them she was drenched in sweat, breathing heavily and her aroused body near it's breaking point. Sensing the time was right, I pressed the flat of the blade against her swollen and wet love slit. Pulling back I felt the slave's body convulse and she let out a sharp cry and the resulting orgasm pulsed through her entire body.

I heard applause coming from the lounge, and turned, thrilled to have pleased my mistress. To my mind the story had been perfect; Ricci had been aroused to climax and while the potential of danger had always been present no damage had been done.

"Nicely done my pet; a good performance. However, Ricci is not some Compact lady indulging in a slave fantasy. She *is* a slave. You are the one who should be squirting across the podium not her. At the very least you should be climaxing at the same time she does. Bend her to your will, she is your toy. I give you permission to break her so long as you enjoy the experience."

I looked at Lexi not knowing how to proceed. In talking about the dynamics of top and bottom relationship Brutal had always stressed that despite the top's illusion of control it was always the bottom in charge. Now Lexi wanted me to truly take control. And I wasn't sure how to do that.

"Ah I see, pet, you don't know how. Alright where to start," said Lexi thinking.

"Ah! Of course it's so obvious! Release the Blood Princess! Pet, don't think of Ricci as a bottom you must satisfy. Instead think of her as the opponent you must beat. Draw her blood! Forget illusion, make it real. You're the Blood Princess; make her realize what that means, pet.

Once again part of me wanted to run, what Lexi wanted flew against everything that I'd been taught by Brutal. But I wanted to please my mistress. And looking at Ricci I saw a look I was very familiar with because I'd seen it in a mirror when I'd been in her place.

"Take me to the next level," it said. "I can take it, come on, I dare you."

I smiled the way I smiled when I knew that I totally out classed an opponent. I flipped the kopis up into the air and started to walk towards my toy. Her eyes widened with understanding as I quickly stuck out my hand behind my back and caught the razor sharp knife without even looking.

Terror about where the limits were right at that moment crossed her face.

"Well hello Princess I am *so* glad you decided to join us," purred my Mistress.

In a fight I use my whole body as both a weapon and a shield, and this is how I approached my toy. I wrapped my body around her. Always there was some part of my body in direct contact with my toy, hands, breasts, stomach, or inner thigh. All were in contact at some point. The constant connection and the energy that my toy gave off was intoxicating and for the first time ever the visceral emotions of battle were mixed with the aroused feelings of sex as battle lust mixed with true lust.

Much as before I drew the kopis blade over the toy's skin only this time stimulating the areas where she was weakest: her breasts of course, and her inner thighs and groin. But also behind her knees and strangely from my perspective the nape of her neck. Again I'd draw the knife with the grain of her skin only then I'd often reverse the direction of the knife and break the skin leaving a long line welling with blood.

Time went on, and I paused took a step back and examined my toy. From the neck down there were a score of shallow cuts or punctures. In some the blood had welled up and mixed with my toy's sweat causing small rivulets of blood to trickle from the wound. But like any good fighter I had not just attacked with my weapon. Her back had finger nail scratches deep enough to have drawn blood. Her right shoulder and her upper left breast had bruising where I'd bitten hard enough to leave a mark. But despite having cried out in pain many times my toy was glassy eyed; lost in the pleasure of the stimulation that the pain provided.

But it wasn't just her. I'd never been this aroused; had never allowed my desire to build to this level of intensity. It felt like every nerve in my body was firing at the same time. Gasping as if there was no good air I looked down upon my own body. I realized that my own sweat had mixed with the toy's blood and smeared across my body. Once again the Blood Princess was truly present.

"*Time to finish this fight,*" I thought to myself.

Moving up, I once again embraced my toy. My lips found her ear and I whispered "Time to see who breaks first."

I then drove the flat edge of my kopis hard up onto my toy's burning loins and ran it back and forth between her pussy lips and over her clit. Any screams that she would have made were muted as I drove my tongue down her throat in a frenzied kiss. I pressed our breasts together so hard that it caused one set of our nipple rings to become locked. And I ground my own pussy hard against her thigh matching the pace that I set with my battle blade.

Given the state that both of us were in right then, neither of our bodies could resist such machinations for long. My toy's body then lock up as her entire body arched back in climax. This was all the stimulation that my own body could endure and I also screamed in exalted ecstasy. Our legs were soaked with our cum and the only reason why we didn't collapse onto the floor was that my toy was chained and I hung onto her for dear life.

I'm not sure how long had passed before my over stimulated body could once again receive information about the outside world. But when it did, my mistress was up standing beside both my toy and I, pulling the sweat soaked hair back away from our faces so that she could see our expressions.

"Much better, pet. Much, much better," my mistress said approvingly.

She was completely naked as well, and a third of the overseer rod in her hand was soaking wet.

"I always knew that you had it in you to take control of someone else in such a way," she said, standing next to me, her right hand cupping my right butt cheek, thumb outlining the brand that was there.

"Know this, my pet. Ricci will never feel as grateful to anyone as she does to you right now. You forced her into experiencing a painful, terrifying, situation and you showed her how to take that situation and take great bodily pleasure from it,"

My toy looked up at our Mistress and nodded in agreement to what she was saying.

Turning to speak to my toy directly our mistress asked, "Do you wish to preserve that experience so that you will never have to stop feeling that way for the rest of your life Ricci?"

"Yes please mistress this slave would love to always feel this way." Was my toy's...Ricci's... reply.

"You heard her pet. Does the slave deserve to be rewarded? It is in your power to do so,"

"Yes mistress she does deserve a reward. How do I grant it to her?" I asked.

"Simple, pet, embrace her once more. Kiss her with passion again. And either slit her throat or drive your knife hard up into her heart. She will then die blissfully knowing that you gave her the ultimate slave death. The pleasure of knowing that with her last moments upon this earth, she not only gave great pleasure to her owner, but also that she had such a generous master as to be allowed to feel such pleasure herself."

I looked at my toy and saw that she was in complete agreement with our Mistress. Death would be the ultimate stimulant.

My left hand entwine into my toy's hair, as I started to fulfill her last request. It was then that I felt a sharp burning pain in my lower back, and the little voice in the back of my head started to speak with greater volume.

"Why are you referring to the little teen wannabe twit as your mistress? Her mother was from house Hector. Why have you broken Brutal's cardinal rules of the top/bottom relationship so quickly? When did she see Brutal and you together in one of Brutal's stories? Why have you dehumanized Ricci by thinking of her as your toy: She's human? Who else has called you pet? And last but not least, Lexi's hand on your ass, her thumb isn't tracing out your current brand but the shape of the original brand.

It was like being hit with a bucket of ice cold water. I suddenly realized who had been here all along. Swiftly I snap kicked Lexi in the centre of her chest, sending her flying back to the far side of the building. I then sprinted to the other side of the room and grabbed up my other kopis.

"Get out of my head Hector," I snarled.

Everything that happened, the only thing that made sense was Hector. The former leader of House Hector, the vampire who had me and a friend branded as part of an off world trade agreement. The bastard that I had turned to ash. The creature that I knew had been hounding my dreams for weeks.

Lexi was getting up and there was no hiding it now. Gone was any femininity to the body language or even her facial features.

"Well met, Blood Princess, I must admit I am surprised that you were able to overcome my influence. You have been the only one so far to recognize the ruse, and some of those I have been in contact with have been alive and playing our games for centuries," the vampire said admiringly.

"How?" was my only reply. Well my only verbal reply. I constantly moved. Keeping a sharp eye on Hector's vessel, I moved to Ricci and with one swift stroke of my right hand kopis cut through the bindings on one of her wrists.

"Can you free yourself from here?" I asked the slave in a quiet voice.

Glassy eyed and still recovering from what had been done to her, Ricci was still able to nod positively.

"How I am talking through this girl? How are you able to resist? How is it that I'm still here? What, my pet, you have to be clearer in your question," he said clearly, enjoying himself.

That didn't reassure me though. While true that if he was playing with his food this way it meant that he wasn't planning on attacking just yet, that didn't mean that I wasn't out of the woods. My defeat of Hector last time had been a matter of luck and desperation. There was no way I could match him right now.

"How is it that you're possessing my miss...Lexi's body. I knew you were alive from my dreams. Not very subtle by the way," I said. Hells no sense in not getting my own digs in while I could.

"All part of a master plan, my dear, to secure this city under my control. A plan which you played your part in beautifully, I might add."

"So having your contracts declared null and void, your house destroyed and your family members thrown into the great maw of the Compact, not to mention your physical body destroyed was all part of a master plan?" I asked in total confusion. Either this Hector was the most manipulative far-sighted bastard on the planet or he was bat shit crazy.

I was leaning towards the latter.

"Yes, and you played your part beautifully as well, my pet, very convincing." He said with a smile.

"I was trying not to become some elemental's fuck toy Hector, there was no acting on my part. I was trying to kill you," I replied. Yup bat shit crazy.

"You don't get it, Blood Princess; those 'contracts' those 'Compacts' not only bind the house's actions but us as well. The chaos lords, the astral masters and the demon princes all know that you have to bind the mortal not his words. With the 'destruction' of House Hector, I and all of mine are now truly free," he paused seeing that once Ricci had freed herself I moved her back to the pegs where my equipment was hung.

"Oh, is the sex part over? You have to forgive me, for all her talk the girl has had little experience and to be honest it's been a few centuries since I was young enough to be interested in the rituals of seduction. I assume things have changed since then,"

"Yes Hector, the sex part is over," I said firmly. Ricci was behind me, seemingly recovered from her sexual climax but still confused by the sudden turn of events.

"Oh, pity, I have to admit both Lexi and I were enjoying the show. I have to thank you for the opportunity for experiencing sex from the woman's perspective. Being as old as I am truly new experiences are a rare treasure," he said as he moved to don his own clothing.

"I'm afraid to ask, but what happens now?" I asked before I put one of my kopis between my teeth and another balanced upon the top of my foot. Hector knew from personal experience just how quick I could get a weapon from my foot to my hand. I then slipped on my panties. Without even being asked Ricci took the silk underwear and pulled them into place.

"Let me do this you keep an eye on whatever has control of mistress," whispered Ricci.

Hector seemed nonplused by our actions as he/she got dressed. "We leave, I buy Ricci and we return home so that you fulfil your contract. Then I hire you again from a different body and we continue with your education. You are like a wild animal which I intend to tame, not *break* my pet, tame and then groom to be worthy of your name. This was just a test to see how much it is going to take," replied Hector. Was he on the level?

Hector then smiled at me, with a smile I've only ever seen on men. I was his possession and no one, not even the gods themselves could say differently. Perhaps that was the closest thing the old vampire could feel to love.

I guess I was supposed to be flattered, I'd become the obsession of a man centuries old. Who in theory could have had picked anyone.

Fortunately for what little remained of my sanity, the floor exploded upwards, and we were in the process of being attacked.

# Chapter Four

Through the hole came a dozen Naga. Well actually it was a dozen of their brain addled human minions, but they were bad enough.

"There sssshe issss take the fammmily memmmber, kill the ressst," said the hooded leader in the back to the others.

Now the human minions of the Naga worship the Snake Lord, and see the Naga as his angels. As they progress through the ranks of the cult they become more and more like snakes. These guys looked like they've been worshipping the Snake Lord for a while now. But still…

"Seriously guys, some of you still have your hair and you're speaking with lisps? Just how big a group of ass lickers are you?"

A dozen pairs of angry eyes turned my direction. Which is exactly what I wanted them to do.

You see, the blatant desire to be attacked by enemies is the main source of the stereotype of fighters being stupid.

"Hector if you got some mind mojo left now would be the time to use it," I said as I took one calming breath and started to advance towards the closest snake man.

"Annie what's happening? Why are we inside?" asked Lexi. Of course the evil immortal vampire chose this time to leave me with a totally useless Compact princess!

"Ricci get your mistress out of this room, I'll deal with these slimy bastards," I replied.

Yes I know snakes aren't slimy but I'm trying to keep them focused on me so hey; insults.

As Ricci moved, three of the wantabes moved to grab her. This was just what I was waiting for. I turned from the guy I was watching and spirited into the three that were looking the wrong direction.

I cut the hamstring of one with a low cut of my left hand kopis as I passed. The second took a similar slash with my right hand knife. The third I simply drove my shoulder into his solar plexus knocking the wind out of him and driving him to the floor. I rolled from the hit and was back on my feet quickly enough to see the surprised look of everyone in the room.

"Hello, Blood Princess, what were you expecting?"

"Kill…" Started the hooded one in the back, but I never did find out who he wanted killed; because a bolt of arcane energy hit him square in the head and sent him spinning.

Susa! My damned little warlock had to be here. How I wasn't sure, but I'd figure that later. Now I was just glad that she was here.

You can therefore understand my confusion when I turned to thank Susa and instead saw Ricci standing there, Lexi on her knees behind her mouth agape, holding a vicious looking black steel battle sword in two hands pointed towards the snakemen. The blade crackled with the same kind of arcane energy that had taken out the hooded leader.

"Christ I can't believe that worked," said the silver haired slave. She then took a very solid ready stance between the snake men and Lexi. Who looked as if she was past panic and starting to enter denial. My little princess then in an almost perfect image of the helpless female of story, grabbed onto one of Ricci's thighs for protection.

The snake men looked back and forth between the two of us, and hesitated.

"Who's next?" I asked spinning my blades up into the air with easy practise.

I felt the air behind me move and without thinking raised both of my fighting knives up in a cross defence and caught a downward stroke of a serrated short sword between the two of them. I twisted my blades to force the blade to my left and my body flowed with the movement. So I only caught part of the other short sword that was thrust towards where my kidneys had been. Still the hit was enough to open a four inch cut that scraped across one of my ribs.

Hissing with pain I continued my twist to the left. Once I could safely retreat without a counter thrust I released my opponent's blade and step back to face my new attacker.

There before me larger than life was a full-fledged Naga. About 15 feet in total length the Naga was a massive creature of solid flesh. Snakelike in appearance, it still possessed a very masculine set of arms and shoulders, sprouting from a very human appearing torso. Its stomach and the lower part of the snake body was a deep green in colour which lightened and turned into a dirty yellow on its back. Seeing that I knew what it was, the Naga rose up as high as the ceiling would allow. Its chest and shoulder muscles flared like a cobra's hood. His arms were outstretched and he held a wavy stabbing short sword in each. I realized that standing in the centre of the room his reach was almost 6 feet aside.

It was one of those displays that a male fighter would describe as 'dick shrinking'. Fortunately I don't have a dick so I wasn't too impressed. I mean being a woman I've constantly been hit by the male physical intimidation trick. I've killed most of the bastards that tried this trick on me. So they've lost a lot of their impact.

"You pathetic fools! Get the girl while I deal with this mongoose," the Naga shouted to its followers.

"Lexi! Ricci! One of you! Get to the door and shout Fire!" I shouted without my eyes leaving the snakeman.

I've never fought a creature without legs before and its body language was throwing me. Normally I watched my opponent's body for the tells of where and when said opponent will strike. Some will tell you that you should always watch an opponent's eyes for such signs, but I've faced far too many creatures (cough Hector cough) whose eyes were far more dangerous than any weapon on hand.

"It is futile. You will be long dead before your pathetic pleas for help will be answered," said the Naga as it slithered between myself and the other two girls. I turned my own body keeping the two of us in relatively the same position.

So I had a clear view of Ricci's naked body as it became wrapped in living flame. "Then let's give them a real fire to deal with then," she shouted as she cleaved the air in front of her with the sword. The fire leaped from her body down the sword and out before her in a wide swath. All the snakemen showed great survival instincts by trying to leap out of the way. Those that succeeded were gravely wounded but still alive. Those that didn't, fell to the ground, fire rapidly turning them to ash. Once again the little slave girl had checked the advance of the snakemen.

Even the Naga was distracted as it felt the wave of heat wash out behind it. Curiosity must have gotten the better of the snakeman and it risked a quick look behind it. Not waiting for it to turn its head back towards me, I struck. Once again I hit it both high and low at the same time, but the creature was ready and caught each of my blades with one of his. It then lashed out with its head trying to sink its snake fangs into flesh. I was ready for that trick and rolled my body closer to it so that its fangs missed my shoulder by a hair's breath.

What I was not ready for was the long tail. By moving closer I actually played into the Naga's plan. Before I could react the bastard had an eight inch thick coil wrapped around my upper body pinning my arms to my sides, further coils wrapped around hips and legs, pinning me in a scaly death grip. To make matters worse, one of the coils rested between my legs and rubbed against my still aroused vulva and clitoris.

"To end a creature's life amidst the throes of orgasm adds greatly to the taste of the meat. I urge you to relax and let it happen. It is a most pleasurable way to die," said the Naga as if our fight was over.

Yeah, like 'relax and just let it happen' has ever stopped a woman from fighting for her life.

While the Naga and I fought, Lexi had decided to rejoin the world and had gotten up and made a beeline to the door. She opened it and started to shout 'FIRE' at the top of her lungs. She also had the sense to step outside and put a nice thick wall between herself and the battle going on inside.

Lexi's movement had spurred the snakeman back into action and the remaining half a dozen moved towards the door. Only to be intercepted by Ricci. As a general rule, spell casters aren't that big into hand to hand combat. Even Susa who had no fear of being up-close and personal doesn't use it as her first choice.

Ricci, on the other hand, tore into the snakemen with her sword with a gusto that would have made any berserker proud. Still partially clad in flame, she cleaved one of the snakeman's head into two, with one sizzling stroke of the sword and kicked the body off the blade. Whatever Ricci was, her powers were similar to those wielded by Susa. While she'd gotten one she was still badly outnumbered, the Naga's followers pressed forward. Being naked, she soon sported several deeper cuts then the ones I had caused during our knife play. But each time someone hit her, she laughed, and the new flames lashed out burning the attacker.

So my charge was clear, the mystery slave seemed to be holding her own, and I was literally in the clutches of the bad guy. Not the best reference for a bodyguard. The Naga having dealt with me for the moment did a half roll and twist to observe the battle. The manoeuvre nearly dislocated my shoulder and did succeed in bringing about a series of fresh pains to my body and new desires to my pussy. I tried to get one of my arms free but its grip was too tight.

"Must I do everything myself?" asked the Naga in frustration. Moving back into the centre of the room the man snake bypassed the fight between its minions and Ricci and moved directly towards the door. Outside I could still hear Lexi screaming fire at the top of her teenage lungs.

I was starting to get a bit frantic; I wasn't able to get any leverage to free myself, in fact the only part of my body I could move was my head and neck. The coils around me tightened even more. I wasn't able to breathe, and my vision was starting to tunnel.

Well desperate times can lead to desperate ideas and one suddenly hit me.

Not quite believing what I was about to do, I turned my head and bit hard into the snake's soft upper body.

Biting as deep as I could I tore out as large a chunk from its body as I could. Spitting the piece of snake out I tried to bite the monster again.

I must have bitten into a sensitive spot, because the Naga screamed and for a second its grip loosed enough that I was able to get a breath in. With the fresh air powering my body I was able to right myself and get my feet back onto the ground. Suddenly it turned backed to look at me.

"You hairless mongoose! How dare you resist," it bellowed towards me.

"Ah come on, friction is what makes it fun," I smiled my sluttiest smile at it.

I had its attention and I wanted to keep it. It allowed the rest of its tail to slide from me and behind it so that it could once again rise up to the ceiling and execute another diving attack.

Which was exactly when Lia made her move. On hearing Lexi's screams, my quasi sister had come out of her hiding place to land next to our charge and took a peek inside. (Her sharp Elf eyes had no trouble seeing into the room despite the gloom thankfully.)

Seeing things not going well, Lia had timed her attack to when the Naga had been distracted. Then, with a running start, she leaped into the air over Ricci's fight with the snakemen minions and onto the shoulders of the Naga, driving both of her foot long daggers up to their hilts.

The creature roared in pain and convulsed as he rolled onto his back, trying to crush his new attacker under its bulk.

But Lia was far too quick for him. Kicking off the creature, she vaulted to a place behind the humanoid snakemen who were startled by the sudden roar of pain from their master.

With a series of spinning strikes Lia once again struck, crippling two more minions with slashes to their groins.

That's Lia for you, why cause chaos and panic to just one person when you can affect a whole crowd.

Seeing my chance, I moved towards the Naga's head and arms. It still hadn't quite realized that Lia was no longer on its back and was trying to reach behind and grab its tormentor. This left him vulnerable to his real threat.

I moved up and drove the tip of my kopis deep into the creature's arm pit, severing veins, arteries, muscle, and sinew as I pulled the curved fighting knife towards me, half severing the foot thick arm in a spray of bright red blood. The spray, of course, hit me square in the chest, covering me in bright red snake blood.

This potentially-mortal injury was enough for the big monster. Letting out a long wail of pain the creature dove back into the hole and left with a series of hissing cries.

The other snakeman decided that this seemed like a good idea, and the remainder who could, followed their scaly leader down the hole.

"Right, time for us to leave as well," I said to the two other girls, as I moved to put myself between the hole and them.

"Oh fuck yeah," said Ricci with a literal gleam in her eye. The flames played out over her body, but the black iron battlesword was still held firmly.

"Lia, go out and see to our princess while I grab the rest of my stuff," I said.

"You're going to have to explain why you're half naked and just had sex when were done," replied Lia with a smirk.

Lexi to her credit was still just outside the door breathing hard with a wild look in her eyes. It was clear that she was having difficulty trying to understand what was happening to her. When she saw me and Ricci run out covered in blood, her mind shut down completely and she fainted dead away.

"Of course," I said as I sheathed the kopis and lifted the teen over my shoulder.

Then turning to Ricci I said, "You're bought. Do you know the way to the horse stables?" I said to Ricci.

"Yes," was her reply.

"Good, lead the way," I said motioning her to move.

"What in the nine hells is going on," asked Lia. She had fallen in beside me and was literally running backwards, keeping an eye on our rear, as fast as I was running forward under Lexi's extra weight.

"Hector is still alive, he's in love with me, and we got attacked by a Naga's kidnapping ring that wasn't expecting a sex slave to be able to fire bolts of magical energy or wield a three foot long magic battlesword,"

"And you had sex," added Lia. She then glanced back at the welts on my ass cheeks and said "pretty tame sex by your standards, but still."

"Later," I said. We were getting close to Lexi's carriage. Ricci, seeing our destination, let go of her battlesword which disappeared in a puff of sulfurous smoke. Fortunately for them Lexi's entourage was waiting in the carriage. They scrambled aside as I literally threw Lexi on board. All three started asking questions at once.

"See to your mistress!" I ordered in a firm voice. "Lia stay here with them. I'm going up top to make sure that our path stays clear."

Grabbing the top of the open window I pulled myself out of the interior of the carriage and onto its roof.

Watching to the rear I breathed a sigh of relief and took a moment for myself as it became apparent that the coast was clear.

"Mistress," said a voice below me.

I turned and saw Ricci balancing herself on the carriage's door.

"Your friend said you would need these." She said as she past up my armour, a healing potion a skin of brandy wine and a damp towel. (I love Lia's bag of holding and the thousand and one useful items it holds)

"Thank you. Now get back inside." I said to Ricci.

With a pleased smile the little mystery girl disappeared back into the carriage.

# Chapter Five

I didn't start to relax until we passed the gates of the Merath manor house. Even before we exited the carriage, the house guards were over to us. Maybe seeing me riding on top of the carriage with the horses lathered was a tip off. They grabbed Lexi and hustled her and her entourage, now including Ricci, deep into the house. The chamberlain had been called, and he firmly but politely demanded, that Lia and I follow him. Her ladyship wanted an explanation.

So once again we were in the presence of the family matron, only this time she was joined another woman who was content to stay in the shadows.

"Heads up, I can't see her face," whispered Lia as she gently nodded her head towards woman in shadow.

That concerned me. If Lia's Elf eyes were having a problem seeing into simple shadows that could only mean that our mystery woman was using magic to keep her privacy.

The tells that Her Ladyship were giving were even more of puzzlement. All these high end merchant types really try and keep their facial features difficult to read. They're less careful with body language, and it's body language that I watch mostly. I mean you don't know when someone coming at you with a knife by how he smiles.

I was expecting Her Ladyship's body to show anger at her descendant being put into a dangerous situation. Instead I got the distinct impression of relief and more than a little sexual excitement.

Lia noticed it to and we both tensed. Wrong emotional states were a big warning sign in our business.

"I see everyone returned more or less intact," started the Matron. "I presume that this young lady is one of your famed Black Bitches, Princess?"

"Yes, she was providing backup in case something went wrong," I replied.

"And something went wrong, I take it?" asked the Matron.

"Nothing I couldn't handle," was my reply.

"Were there any casualties?" asked the hidden woman. Her voice had a seductive tone to it. Under normal circumstances it would have been pleasurable, even arousing, to listen to. Having just been mind fucked by Hector however meant that her voice just set me on edge.

"I'm sorry, but who are you? And in what capacity do you speak for my employer?" I challenged.

"Ooooh, the Princess has teeth, and integrity I see. Let's just say that I represent parties allied with the Meraths for now," said the hidden woman.

"She is fully in my confidence surrounding this incident, Princess, what you can say to me you can say to her," replied Her Ladyship.

"Very well; everyone who was with your granddaughter is safe and sound. Lexi is a little confused about events and should be allowed to rest for a few days."

"Thank you for your healer's opinion but what happened?" asked the hooded woman.

I took a deep breath; this was not going to be easy. I believe in keeping to the truth when reporting to employers; at least the ones not stabbing me in the back. It's easier than trying to remember which lies I told to which group. But that didn't mean that it was easy.

"She was possessed for several hours by the ghost of one of her ancestors," I said.

"Oh. Who?" asked Her Ladyship as if this were a common occurrence.

"Hector from House Hector. I believe that they're related on her mother's side,"

"Yes, they are. So what did the old bastard want with Lexi?" asked the Matron.

"As far as I could tell he wanted to give her a reputation as a shrewd trader. He was largely successful. Even your accountant was impressed," I replied.

"Interesting," said the grey haired matron, then turning to the cloaked being she asked, "Thoughts?"

"He's making them appear useful, getting them noticed. We both know that the average family member is as useful as tits on a bull. Anyone who starts to stand out will eventually be given more responsibility,"

"Or assassinated by rivals," said Her Ladyship with a degree of cynical disgust that made me like the old crone.

"Then they weren't lucky or good enough to begin with in the first place. But the important thing is that he showed his hand early. I knew he couldn't resist the bait."

Everyone (including Lia, the bitch) turned and looked at me like I was cheese in a rat trap.

"So what does the Master want from us?" asked Her Ladyship to the cloaked figure.

"We'll talk about that later during your reward," said the cloaked figure in a voice full of sexual promise. "For now, leave us; I need to talk to the Blood Princess about our investment in her."

Her Ladyship turned to leave. She moved with the difficulty of one who was highly aroused with no quick release.

Once Lia and I were alone with the mystery guest did she start to move out of the shadows. It was then I saw the bat like wings and the long thin tail with its barbed end. We were talking to a succubus, and it was then I realized just how much danger we were truly in.

"Please sit, ladies; I wish this to be a conversation of equals," the succubus started to say only to be interrupted by the daggers that Lia and I instinctively threw at it. I missed with mine but Lia's hit centre mass.

An overreaction? Devils of any sort are trouble and a succubus just wanting to 'talk' was being hostile.

The succubus disappeared and its voice came from our side.

"Peace, Blood Princess, I'm here to talk about our shared problem not…" the invisible Devil started but it was cut off as Lia threw three of the her throwing spikes in the voice's general direction. The cut off speech and short shriek of pain indicated that at least one struck home.

"Fine! Let's do it your way then," said the succubus.

Lia and I drew our fighting daggers and stood back to back trying to figure out where the next attack would come from. I was eyeing the glass windows, wondering if we could smash through them and survive the jump to the gardens below.

Then I felt a set of wet lips kiss my cheek. And suddenly I was having problems trying to remember why I was so concerned.

"Now sit down both of you I'm not here to fight anyone!" the succubus said with that pleasant voice again.

Sitting down still didn't sound like a good idea, but I did lower my fighting knives. She had such a nice voice and if she didn't want to fight why were they out? I looked over to Lia; she appeared to agree and lowered her weapons.

"Alright, don't sit, but I will," said the succubus dropping the invisibility as it sat down on a large couch. The Devil flapped out her wings and took up the entire piece of furniture.

"Now sheathe your weapons. I don't want to call the guards, but I will if I have to. One way or another we are going to have a discussion about Hector and the threat that he poses to this city," she said her pleasant voice suddenly turning so hard it could have cut glass.

Lia and I sheathed our blades and just stood there in silence, not really sure what to say.

"Finally, some progress. Susa told me you were stubborn and dangerous but really," she said her voice pleasant again.

I suddenly found that statement funny. "Susa would tell you jack shit, Devil," I said snorting.

Susa might look like she was made of paper but she was the toughest most stubborn being I have ever known.

"My name is Liltha. Not Devil, Blood Princess, and while I agree with your assessment, I know Susa better than she knows herself," she said in that same pleasant voice.

Have you ever seen someone you care about in the grips of a night terror? Screamed with such raw terror and pain, that the sound now haunts your dreams? Felt helpless as the only thing you could do once you manage to slap them awake is to hug them, as they cry like a child and cling to you like you are the only thing that is real to them?

I have. With Susa.

And every time it has happened there has been a name on her lips. One name, a name whose owner I have sworn to kill if ever I met *it*: Liltha, the name of the succubus who used torture and rape as a means of magical instruction.

I know it sounds strange to say on one hand that she's the toughest bitch in the City of Gates and on the other that I've held her like a child while she cried herself back to sleep. But that's people. Hit any of us the right way and we'll shatter into a thousand pieces.

Hit us another way and you'll temper us into a whole different person.

Lilthia had just given me the strength to shatter whatever control it had on me thanks to the rage that I now felt.

I ignored its pleasant voice. Hells I forgot it was even talking, as I literally saw red. The next thing I remember my two kopis were hitting the couch, the magically tempered steel cleaving through solid oak and horse hair to meet in where the bitch's heart had been just a fraction of a second before.

I pulled out the knives destroying the couch and sprung back wildly looking around for the Devil. Lia just looked at me stunned, never before had she seen me react in such a blind rage.

It was only then that I felt a rope snake around my neck cutting off my air as two hands encircled mine holding my knives rigid away from my body.

"All I wanted was a nice conversation! But no; you had to do this the hard way. Very well, but know that this is now on your shoulders!" hissed the Devil in my ear.

It was about that time that the house guards entered the room along with Her Ladyship.

"Grab the Elf! I can't control them both!" shouted the Succubus.

To make its point, I rocked my head back and nailed its nose. The Devil screamed as I felt bone break. I also felt, what I now figured out was her tail, around my neck loosen enough for me to draw a breath. I flexed my arms but they were still held rigid in the succubus's grasp.

The guards moved to grab Lia who continued to just stand there under the Devil's influence. House Merath's grey haired Matron, wanting to help her ally, came up to me holding her own overseer's baton in both hands and struck me across the stomach. I think she was trying to knock the wind from me. But I've taken hits from orcs with maces to the abdomen so her blow hardly even registered. I continued to struggle against the Devil's grip.

Grabbing Lia's arms the guards immediately pinned them back and started to bind them. But the succubus interceded first.

"Strip her first, I want to make sure we got any hidden weapons off them. Then hang her by arms with her feet barely touching the floor," said the Devil regarding Lia.

"As for this one…" it whispered in my ear.

Suddenly my arms and legs felt very light as if I was floating. The tail unwound around my neck and I tried to turn and attack the succubus again. Only my arms wouldn't respond as it applied the full force of its mental control over me.

"Strip, Blood Princess! We are going to have our talk but it's going to be the way I usually talk with you soul bags," it said, her voice so full of rage that Her Ladyship paled visibly.

I was fighting the control every second, but my hands moved on their own, taking off my weapons and armour. But the devil's control was costing it. Liltha had broken out in a sweat and it was breathing hard. The Devil was also in pain, its perfect nose was broken and bleeding. Its left wing was also half severed. Apparently my surprise attack had managed to wound her.

Once I was naked, the guards bound my arms together behind my back. While this was going on I saw Lia was being hung from one of the room's rafters. She looked at me as if to say "this is entirely your fault".

"Now then, Blood Princess, I think it's time I introduce you to Susa's punishment position," said Liltha as it approached me with a pair of sharpened steel hooks, attached to what appeared to be a long silk rope.

Throwing one end of the rope over a rafter she handed that end to one of the guards.

"You're a protector, aren't you, Blood Princess," said Liltha with a smile. It then pierced my right nipple with one of the hooks, digging around a bit to make sure that when it poked through the top of the nipple it was under my nipple ring.

I locked my jaw, it hurt like the Nine Hells but I was not going to make a sound to satisfy this bitch.

"Ready to strike down the being that hurt your lover so? I would have expected that from the cleric but never you," it continued as it ran the other hook through my left nipple, making sure once again that it ran under the metal of my nipple ring.

"You hate me because you perceived what I did while training Susa as evil," continued Liltha, as casual as if we'd been talking over a glass of wine. It then signalled the guards and I felt the thin silk rope rise. Intuitively I rose onto my tip toes to keep the pressure off of my nipples.

"But look at the weapon I forged: Strong, driven, resourceful, and fearless in the face of the true horrors of this world. I was even merciful enough to leave her imperfect. Why else would she have those bad dreams?"

I then felt something hit the back of my feet, again they moved instinctively trying to keep the pressure off. Finally I'd found myself wobbling on the balls of my feet on two 6 inch wood dowels. My legs spread wide and very exposed.

"Why else would she cry out my name like a lover caught in an orgasmic embrace?" said Liltha finally as it pulled back fully in my view again.

The bleeding had stopped. Its nose once again looked perfect and her wing was once again whole, though with a barely perceptible scar where my blade had slashed it. Liltha then took a breath and once again I had control over my limbs. Then turning its back to me once more Liltha move over to a large plush chair and sat down. "Now we can finally talk, Blood Princess. That's all that I wanted to do today with you is talk."

"That's like an orc saying that he only wants to spar. He might mean it at the time but it ends up with the orc trying to kill you," I said as evenly as possible. The last thing I wanted to do is let her know just how much pain I was feeling in my breasts and legs.

Liltha gave me a disapproving look. "Do I have to gag you as well Blood Princess? I have tried to show you nothing but courtesy and you and your companion have only reacted with violence.

"Can't blame us for wanting to keep the mode of conversation in an area where we excel, can you?" I asked.

"Annie would you stop poking the cat; you're not helping," said Lia, speaking up for the first time. "Let's hear what it has to say while we play for time and look for an opportunity to get out of here with our skins intact."

Liltha looked at Lia an expression of surprise on its face. "That is a most blunt and honest assessment my dear, I commend you," it said to Lia.

"Oh please, can we skip the chess game, and second guessing? You have the advantage. We know what that means and how you are going to react. And we are at a disadvantage, and you know how we are going to react. Can you two stop your pissing match over Susa and get to what in the Nine Hells is the point!" said the Elf in exasperation

I swear on the Sun God's shiny balls that Liltha actually looked embarrassed.

"Well I guess *we've* been told," The succubus said to me.

"Very well Lia I shall get to the point, as you say. Which is this. All of you are in grave danger."

"Tell us something we don't know bitch," I said as I nearly lost my balance and felt a sharp tug on my breasts.

"Annie," hissed Lia in a warning tone.

"It's okay my dear, I have to consider how high strung she is when I hear her responses," said the Devil.

*"Oh great she's torturing me with puns now,"* I thought to myself.

"Okay we're in grave danger; I take it you're talking about Hector?" I instead said in as civil a matter as I could.

"In large part yes; but not entirely. When you destroyed House Hector and openly displayed the hypocrisy of the Compact, you did more to disrupt the status quo within the city than everyone else had in the rest of the cities history combined," answered the Devil

"The minor merchant families saw that a major Compact house could be taken out. That the vaunted security that the Compact law was supposed to provide was a sham. You also showed the Compact Families that they could take each other over, which is something that the true leaders of this city have spent centuries trying to prevent. In other words, people are waking up from their orgies and blood sports and realizing what true power looks like. But most importantly; by not providing the tribute, the Compact itself has been broken. A minor break to be sure, but enough to allow other parties a way into this city."

Liltha smiled "That means that for the first time in centuries, new opportunities are opening up, and many 'Interested Parties' are seeing a chance to get more of the prize. Including your own precious Sun God by the way.

"Now along with their plans within plans and secret agendas and new alliances people in the know are keeping an eye on the Blood Princess and her Black Bitches," she added with a smirk.

"Why us?" asked Lia for both of us.

"For whatever reason, you four are odds breakers. The exception to the rules, the lucky penny, whatever you want to call it," Liltha looked very serious almost fearful.

"Those of us who have existed long enough have seen your kind before. You're god makers, demon slayers, world destroyers, for good or ill you bring the plague of change and it's only a question of who you will infect."

The Succubus then smiled as the fear passed.

"Some think that it's possible to control such forces, and one who believes so has allied with Hector. The vampire has made a pact with the Master of Secrets. And from his display today the one whom I serve now knows the power that pact gives him and what his play is. He also appeared to have become quite obsessed with you Blood Princess. I'd even go so far to say he's in love with you but I doubt he even remembers what that emotion feels like."

"Great so to sum up, you're saying we're some sort of godslaying super women and the ghost of a centuries old vampire is so in lust with me that he wants to reshape me into the image of his idea woman. This while the very gods themselves are looking on trying to figure out which one of them I'm going to kill,"

I then looked down at my position which Liltha had me in and followed up by saying "No offence but I just can't see it,"

"They're not worried about which one you're going to kill they're worried about which one you're going to replace. Remember, the God of War was once just a mercenary, and the Black Lady of Winter was once the Death God's fuck toy. Those who change the world start by being forged by it, Blood Princess," replied Liltha.

"Alright, say you're right, why are you telling us?" I asked.

"We are opposed to the Master of Secrets, and by informing you of his pact with Hector we work against his plans and weaken him by exposing the truth. Also, while trying to control one such as you is a fool's game, directing you or shifting your course isn't. I'm aware of Hector's attempts to influence you at night. It's only a matter of time before he succeeds, which means you need more protection. This is why Whom I Serve has arranged for you to have a bodyguard." said Liltha.

"A bodyguard?" I said disbelieving her words. Like I would trust anyone or anything that came from this bitch. I then thought about it for a second and then everything started to fit together.

"Ricci! She's the bodyguard. That explains the brand. You cunt! She's not from this world! She's helpless, open to be exploited in this city. She needs my protection," I started to rage than the cold realization of the Devil hit me.

"Which you knew I'd do regardless. But she's also very capable in the right circumstances."

My anger had shifted my feet a bit and I felt as if I was losing my balance. Swallowing hard I struggled to stay on the wooden doweling. I promised myself when I had the chance, I'd gut this Devil and present its head to both Susa and Ricci as a gift.

"Oh, I understand Hector now: Deadly fighting skills, beauty, brains, a strong sex drive and a pain slut. A being from the dark planes could go centuries before finding another such as you, Blood Princess. If you weren't marked by another I'd try you out right now," said Liltha licking her lips and her eyes suddenly filled with sexual hunger.

But in a flash that look was gone.

"You're right, of course," it continued as if nothing had changed. "Like Susa, Ricci has entered into a covenant with one of us, only one more oriented to hand to hand combat. The One Whom I serve thought that it would be more appropriate for you. Unfortunately she was not as strong as Susa. During her training her mind snapped. The only way to keep her a useful tool was to erase large parts of her memories. There are many things she knows but not why she knows them. I think it adds to her charm," it said casually.

"As we speak, her bill of sale is being transferred to you. You will own her within minutes. Now what you do with her is up to you. Sell her, free her, kill her or fuck her brains out it's your choice. I and the One Whom I serve do not care. It's up to you. But know this, when Hector comes for you tonight, he will have to get through her first, and he will not like what she can do." With that Liltha got up and made a great show of straightening its leather dress. It then said "Well, my master's message and gift have been delivered, so time for me to go,"

The Devil then moved over to where Lia hung. Liltha loosed her bonds letting Lia fall to the floor. The Elf landed gracefully and in a defensive stance, not sure what the Devil now intended.

"Lia, it has been a genuine pleasure. I am sorry that you had to be placed in such an uncomfortable position, but I do have a right to protect myself. Your property is on the table. If you wish I can arrange for you to have some additional time with which to chastise your friend," said Liltha to the Elf.

"No, I'll get back at her at a time and place of my own choosing," replied Lia, with complete honesty.

"I both understand and approve my dear. Could I trouble you with unhooking the Blood Princess after I leave? It would be best for everyone I believe," said Liltha.

"Of course, no problem,"

"Excellent," she said, turning to her attention back to me. "Princess, you will find your fee for today's exceptional service and Ricci waiting for you in the lobby. And if we meet again, I will repay you for the insult today," ended the succubus with a smile that began and ended at its lips.

Once we were alone, I saw Lia relax visibly and take several deep breaths before she shot me a daggered look and then made a big show of turning her back to me while she got dressed.

I knew Lia was pissed at me so I figured that it was better not to say anything until she had a chance to cool down a bit.

Lia was a professional and she was done dressing quickly, then grabbing my weapons and armour she came to where I was hanging.

"On a scale of 1 to 10…" I wasn't able to finish saying how angry are you at me; because Lia nailed me hard in the stomach with her right fist. She'd done it right and put all of her weight behind the blow, all 96 pounds.

Which meant that it did hurt, believe me.

"By all the gods of the Seven Halls of Heaven what were you thinking? I mean; what brilliant insight did you have that made you decide once she had turned us both into puppets but still just wanted to talk to us that you 'oh here's my chance I think I'll attack her again she'll never expect that!'"

"Before I answer that you think you could cut me down?" I asked trying to keep my voice reasonable.

"Oh don't tempt me! I have half a mind to leave you up there and let the Merath have you as their new lamp holder! Or at the very least knock the block from your feet and leave you hanging there."

"Lia!"

"Oh don't worry it wouldn't be worth the nagging I'd get from Gwen," she said as she passed by me and cut the bindings holding my elbows and wrists together.

"Damn close though," she muttered in a stage whisper, as she undid the knot holding the silk rope that kept my breasts suspended upwards.

By then I had already removed one hook. Thank the gods that the hooks weren't barbed so they didn't do any more damage coming out than going in.

Once I was done I walked over to my weapon's belt and removed the healing potion from it secure case.

Downing it I could feel it starting to work almost immediately, as the pain in my breasts subsided along with the cramping in my legs.

Feeling better I started to get dressed. Glancing at Lia I saw she was still looking for an explanation.

"Okay, first off, have you ever been with Susa when she's had one of her night terrors?" I asked my friend.

"Not in the same bed no, but I've heard her go off. Thought we were under attack the first time, couldn't sleep for the rest of the night," replied Lia. "But what does that have to do with the reason you attacked the succubus?"

"Every time she's gone off with either of us, the cause has always been the same, the tortures she suffered while during her time learning to become a warlock.

"Well I guess that makes sense, Gwen talked to me about it the first time it happened. Gwen was really strange, I'd never seen her so full of rage before. Not at Susa but at the creature who did that to her,"

Lia paused for a second finally putting two and two together.

"Wait, you mean that Devil was…"

"Susa's instructor and chief rapist," I answered.

"And believe me when I say I know exactly why Gwen was so enraged. I felt the same way," I said.

"When I heard her name and realized who it was, I just saw red and attacked."

My tone turned iron hard. "You have to see it to believe it Lia. When Susa awakens she's like a child again, so full of pain and fear that she can barely breathe let alone talk. I've had to hold her close and keep my hands over her because I've seen her scratch herself deep enough to draw blood. And all that was caused by the creature that we just had a polite chat with."

Lia was silent for a moment, maybe she understood, but I think she was still pissed.

"Alright," she said at last "what about that other stuff? You believe it about all that God slayer shit?" she asked as I placed my last two throwing knives into their sheaths.

"Oh I'm fairly sure that she's blowing large amounts of sunshine up our asses. But I think it's telling us some truth. We'll have a better idea once we talk to Gwen and Susa about it," I said heading towards the entryway.

"What about Ricci?" asked the Elf.

"Oh she's free and clear as soon as we can get her to the Sun God's safe house and tatted up. The last thing I want today is Gwen chewing my ass off for keeping a slave," I said opening the door.

Liltha was good to her word. In the entry way stood the Merath chamberlain besides a small table on top of which were several stacks of gold coins. To his right was Ricci;

kneeling with legs wide, back straight, head high, shoulders back, gut in and hands behind her back. In the time we'd been with the succubus Ricci had been cleaned up and made presentable. A leash now ran from her clit ring to the chamberlain's hand. And she looked at us with eyes full of anticipation.

As I approached held forth the leash along with a slip of paper which I assumed was Ricci's bill of sale.

"Your property, Blood Princess, and your compensation for today's services. My mistress wishes to pass on her regrets about the subterfuge in regards to our patron. And the subsequent actions we took. We had no choice but to cooperate and hope that this incident does not sour relations between yourself and our family. As a show of good faith my mistress has ordered a public cab to take your party anywhere in the city at our cost," said the chamberlain nervously. The man looked pale and he was sweating for reasons that had nothing to do with the heat.

I decided to put Liltha's words to a bit of a test.

"Please tell your Mistress that I understand the position your patron put you in. I consider the matter to be closed," I said formally.

I saw the chamberlain visibly relax.

I gave Ricci's leash a sharp tug to indicate that she should rise, and then looked the chamberlain hard in the eye.

"However, let your Mistress know, that if she assist in anything like this again, against me or mine, her family will disappear as completely as has House Hector. Do you understand?"

"I will pass on your message Blood Princess," said the Chamberlain all but shacking in fear.

"See that you do," I replied, then turning I left the house without looking back.

Lia and I didn't talk at all until we got into the cab and it was well away from the Merath's front gates.

"They paid us double what we originally agreed to, Annie. I don't know about you, but I think Liltha may have been telling us the truth," said Lia finally.

"Or least the family she's the patron of believes her," I said.

"Do you have a change of clothing in your bag?" I then asked Lia as I reached down and freed Ricci from the leash.

"Several," she replied as she rummaged through her prized bag of holding.

"Here, this should work," said the Elf as she handed me a typical shear slip of a outwall worker.

Taking the slip I handed it over to Ricci.

"Okay here's what we're doing. You're free, understand. I don't want a slave. Now don't worry were going to take you to a safe house for escaped slaves," I said to Ricci.

I showed Ricci the broken chain tattoo on my right leg.

"If we can't get that brand removed then you'll get a tattoo like this one, indicating that you're a free woman. They'll then help you get onto your feet and even out of the city if that's what you wish. You understand all that?" I asked finally.

"Yes," replied Ricci.

"Great, then it's settled," I started.

"No, it's not Mistress," said Ricci.

Both Lia and I looked at the girl puzzled. Then I said.

"You know your right, you actually deserve a 1/3 share of the payment we got today, given how much you helped with the Naga. That's enough to help you get back onto your feet; and like I said you're free so you don't have to call…"

"Keep the money, I mean, no I don't want to be free, I want to stay your slave Mistress."

"You want to stay my…" I stopped I truly did not know what to say.

"I'm not from this world, mistress. Hell I'm not sure I'm from this dimension after everything I've been through. But I know how dangerous this world is. I know how close I was to being sold into a horrible situation. I saw what you did to protect me and that girl, first from that possession then from those snakeman. Right now my best chance to stay alive and reasonably, safe is to stay your property and your responsibility Mistress," said Ricci in a logical dispassionate matter.

She then gave me a beautiful smile full of sexual promise, "Besides, I love your knife play and I'm sure that I can more than satisfy your needs both in and out of bed."

Gwen was going to go apoplectic when she heard this.

"She has a point, Annie; she'll be safer in many ways with you than on her own even with the church. Plus we could use another blade in the group. Not to mention we know that she's Liltha's plant in the group which is more than we'd know if we reject her," said Lia.

"You're enjoying this, aren't you," I said to Lia.

"Just a bit yeah," replied the Elf with a smile.

But Lia's face then turned serious.

"One last thing that still bothering me," she said.

"Oh?" I asked.

"Yeah, there was a point there where I was sure the Devil wanted to fuck your brains out. But it backed off. What did it say, 'been marked by another'? Who's marked you? And when did they do it?" she asked.

"I'll worry about that later," I said, but as I did so I felt a sharp pain in the small of my back, right where the pain had flared when I finally succeed in throwing off Hector's influence. And thinking further about it, that was where Susa had clawed me when I had met Hector for the first time.

One headache at a time I told myself. And right now I had a silver-haired slave girl as my biggest headache.

"Alright, you can stay my servant, but that's it." I told Ricci

"Of course mistress," said Ricci who had folded the slip and placed it on the cab's seat. She then slid still naked onto the cab's floor and assumed the pleasure slave ready position. But not before running the end of her leash over her swollen and wet pussy lips prior to her reattaching it to her clit ring.

Great, I'm the leader of some sort of cosmic change squad. Have a disembodied vampire who's in lust with me. Made a Devil, so skilled in torture it gave my blood thirsty warlock lover nightmares, into an enemy. And to top it all off I have my own personal sex slave who I know is not going to respect my boundaries. Not to mention a judgemental half-sister who is going to make it sound like it's all my fault.

I love my life.

# A Night at the Dark Queen: The Blood Princess Saga Book 3

# Acknowledgements

One again a big thank you to Matt O for copy editing this work. It's a big job well worth the bottle of scotch it cost me.

To Anson: for allowing me to use the image he created as my cover. If you like his work then I'd suggest taking a look at this other pieces at http://anson7.deviantart.com.

This is the last of the first three. My first three stories I had been working on when I decided to take the plunge into writing professionally. My last acknowledgement goes to my parents, upon whose shoulder I stand while I reach for the stars.

Can I say that while at the same time cringe at the thought of them reading this book?

# Chapter 1

For the past 500 years the Compact has kept the peace within the City of Gates. Signed in blood, and witnessed by Gods, the Compact was a peace treaty between the City's major trading families. Up to that point the families had engaged on a multi front war for the possession of this strange section of the world where several stable inter-dimensional gates open and other temporary gates can be opened at much reduced costs in magical energy and material.

At its fundamental level the treaty forbids the signatories, referred to now as the Compact Families, from open conflict. It also set up an alternate dispute resolution mechanism to prevent things from boiling over.

All of which turned the open warfare between the families into a cold war of cloak, dagger, and one-upmanship. And thank the Gods for that, because I'd never find work otherwise.

Yeah, see, the treaty meant that the Compact Families needed groups that they could deny knowing.

'Oh, your warehouse burnt down? Must have been vandals. You think it was us? Prove it.'

Or:

'I understand that you are currently missing your seal? How do I know? Well, this package just showed up on my front door step with your seal in it. I'd be more than happy to return it to for say a 10,000 pieces of gold finder's fee and a public thank you.'

You know, that kind of thing.

This is where we come in.

My name is Annabelle, Annie for short. The Blood Princess is my professionally name. I run a team calling itself the Black Bitches. A bit gaudy I know but it does roll of the tongue and it's not a name you forget easily. Mine is largely a word of mouth referral business so such things are important to stand out.

One thing that almost all employers ask is how I ended up with my title. Most times I give some bullshit answer. Usually about being the last of a long dead royal line and leave it at that. They're happy enough with the romantic fiction; their problem is being solved not by scum but a ne'er-do-well royalty. Employers wanting to keep that fiction don't pry further.

However, some employers ask because they want to know for some esoteric or perceived security reason, and they employ truthsayers. I look these stuffed shirts square in the eye and say "The name resulted from a night of drunken debauchery at the Dark Queen," smile sweetly and say nothing more.

Mentioning the City of Gates most notorious brothel is usually enough. How it enforces its policy of what happens in the Queen stays in the Queen is legendary and no one wants to cross them. That and the truthsayers knowing that I'm speaking the truth drives them nuts.

However there have been a couple of clients who have earned some trust. Usually while passing a joint or over a cup of wine they have politely asked. They just want to know the story for the story's sake.

For those I tell this full and somewhat embarrassing tale.

It was about a year before we took out Hector, when Gwen had just gotten us together as a team.

Yes, it was my half-sister cleric of the Sun God (or Lightbearer, Lightbringer, Torch Carrier whatever name you wanted to give him) that can ultimately be blamed. Gwen had just established herself within one of the Sun God's missions in the slums out wall. This had been her life's goal but now that she had gotten it she was left with the basic question of what next?

She claims to this day that the next logical step was to find out where she had come from so that she could then plan out where she wanted to go. But I still wonder if the Lightbearer had other ideas and did a little divine "inspiration".

Whatever the reason, Gwen went about looking for her parents and with a little divine effort she located her mother's grave. With that clue, her next step was to head to the Compact's House of Records.

Interesting fact: Compact law requires a parent to recognize a bastard before they could disown it. Well those recognitions are part of the public record and kept at the House of Records. Because of the potential amount of money involved, these records are well maintained (not to mention well guarded by both mundane and magical means).

So Gwen had gone to those records and with her mother's name had found out that she had two half sisters. She tracked down both of us and poof: instant family.

You know, family is a curious thing. Even though we were only half-sisters we've all been 'Storm Cursed' by the God of Storms and Physical Challenge (how that combo came about I have no idea). We're all addicted to the rush we get in dangerous situations. Gwen, even though she was running a mission in the out wall slums and was facing down thugs and gang members, wanted to test herself against what she thought were the Light Bringer's true enemies.

Lia was a skilled cat burglar, one of the city's best. But simple theft wasn't enough for her anymore. She wanted face her adversaries to rub her cleverness in their faces.

I was an up and coming pit fighter, who was trying to decide if should be become a full arena gladiatrix, or join a mercenary company and get out of this city. (This had been my original plan in the first place).

Oh in case you're wondering, Susa isn't so much addicted to danger as much as she's dangerous. The rest of us find her intoxicating and this is the reason why she's managed to seduce Lia at least once (I know it's been at least once because she got me at the same time). Still has Gwen wrapped around her finger and keeps me twisting in the wind.

So back to the instant family. Now that we'd found each other, now what? Sensing a need within all three of us to step it up a level, we decided to form a team that could get paid for handling other people's problems for them. Of course starting out we didn't make much, but that turned around after the mission where I also got my professional name, though not for the reason you may think.

It had involved the return of a lost family heirloom to the Serett family. The relic had been stolen by a group of Goblins who had in turn sold it to their Hobgoblin buddies who had almost smuggled it out of the city when we had caught up with them. It had been a glorious fight. One I had ended in a 1 on 1 duel with the Hobgoblin champion. I killed him by a vicious slash to the throat which had caught me in a spray of bright arterial blood (I know surprising for me right). Knowing that I had to make sure I intimidated the rest of the Hobgoblins I had cut off his head and held it up for all to see. The chief decided to agree with our terms and returned the relic, saying that he didn't want to cross the Princess of Blood.

After cleaning up both the relic and me, we returned it to the grateful Seretts, and got paid including an added bounty for the Hobgoblin's champion. It was our biggest payoff by far, and our first bounty. So we did what any problem solver group did when getting their first big payoff: we hit the taverns.

The night had been usual for the City of Gates, hot and humid, as opposed to oppressively hot and humid during the day. When we went out for the tavern run, the others decided that I needed a break from my usual non-armoured clothing of choice.

Okay, I have a bit of a confession. It has only been in the past few months that I've taken an interest in personal care or looks. At the time of this tale, I was rebelling against the city's obsession with feminine beauty.

In part it was simple teenage rebellion. My mother had

been a tavern wench/whore who used both magic and mundane cosmetics to keep her looking years younger than she really was. I didn't want to follow in her footsteps, spread my legs 3 or 4 times a day for strange men, and wait on other strange men at tables the rest of the time.

I was also emulating the people who I did want to be like: the foreign mercenaries who made up most caravan guards. The mercenaries are from all over the world and even from other dimensions. Their appearances are as varied as the languages they speak but there is one thing that they share in common. They come from places colder and drier than the Gates. They dress in leathers and furs, and use chainmail and steel plate for armour.

Okay, I'll grant you some do die of heat stroke. But many just sweat through working here. And while they do stink to high heaven they look incredibly tough, dangerous, and at least to me, incredibly exotic.

But mostly I now believe that I didn't bother about my looks because I felt that I somehow didn't deserve to look good. Added to that was the truth that I didn't have anyone in my life who cared how I looked.

Now I had sisters, a Half Elf and Elf no less. Beauties both, they did genuinely care about how I looked. So that is how that night instead of my usual men's shirt and leather pants I found myself in one of Gwen's silk dresses.

The dress, as befitted a cleric of the Sun God, was a conservative cut for the Gates. But I'm two inches taller than Gwen with a broader build. On me the dress was tight in all the right places, at least according to Susa and Lia. The skirt that ended mid-thigh on Gwen rode up to an inch below my butt cheeks on me. I'd never shown that much leg before and only agreed after a lot of cajoling. Then with a pair of black sandals (flats; I'd never worn heels yet) and matching belt and money bag I was deemed ready for the town.

After being asked to leave our second tavern of choice

tavern due to, ah, 'unladylike behaviour', our group broke up. Gwen begged off due to religious observances. Lia had played the cute clueless blonde Elf card and was currently off with a young Compact boy helping him spend daddy's gold on her. That just left me with Susa.

Ah Susa. It's impossible to briefly describe Susa. She's human, around my age, and a warlock, but that's so inadequate. I guess to start; she's Gwen's best friend, lover, and domme. Two years ago Susa had helped my sister and several others escape slavery, torture, rape, and possibility the spit in a Gnoll camp. The price for that heroic deed had been Susa's soul, literally. A devil had approached her and had entered a convenant with him for a Warlock's Infernal powers in return for her soul. When I asked Gwen how the Sun God felt about her sleeping around with an Infernal Warlock she said in complete honesty "The Lightbringer commands us to seek out darkness and show compassion and mercy." Then with an impish smile which had absolutely nothing to do with religion she added, "Besides, we're good for each other."

The Infernal Covenant had changed Susa both physically and emotionally. Gwen told me that Susa always had pale skin, black hair and dark eyes, but the pact had turned her skin ghostly white and darkened her eyes to jet black. Her choice of clothing, body modifications and make up does nothing but enhance this look, making her one of the most exotic women I know of in a City known for its exotic beings.

As well, Susa is a hedonist; she is very much about living in the moment and extracting as much bodily pleasure that she can from it be it from alcohol, drugs, or sex (especially sex), with no regards for consequences. To her credit she's usually careful whom she takes on these wild rides, and tries to minimize damage beyond herself, but she's not always successful.

The night of the party, she had worn a sheer black

dress that had an open top showing off much of her cleavage. It ended so high on the thigh she constantly flashed crotch and bare ass cheeks just by walking. It was one of the reasons why I agreed to wear Gwen's white dress. With as much skin as it showed I still looked like a conservative old maid next to Susa.

She'd been flirting (Susa flirts the way most women breathe) with everyone that night, but mostly with me. Now normally such blatant sexual attention and the danger it represented have made me feel uncomfortable. But that night: That night I was still on a high from the fight and, well, drunk so the danger Susa represented was intoxicating and I wanted more.

So there you have it. My rational explanation as to why I asked a hedonistic nymphomaniac. "Where's the best place to get some action?" Now you understand why I believe that the Gods curse good people by giving them exactly what they ask for.

Susa's answer to the question was the Dark Queen. Now, the Queen feels like a second home to me, but that night I might have well stepped through one of the cities gates to a new dimension. I'd never seen a place like it. Four stories tall, with the same number of basements, and taking up a full block, the brothel contains among other things: an interior courtyard out of site of the road; at least three secret exits; its own body art/beauty salon, clothing store, three different bars/parlours; many different kinds of bedrooms up to and including full suites, and as I was later to find out a at least one theatre.

We entered The Dark Queen giggling like a couple of preteens who had just caught our older brother naked; a bad sign in my experience. I was surprised when the doorman, a large Human male, gave Susa a polite bow in greeting.

"Evening Susa, we haven't seen you in a while. Where's that little strawberry blonde Half Elf of yours?" he asked in a familiar tone.

"Hey Vince. Gwennie had other things to do tonight, so I settled for her sister," replied Susa in a lustful voice. She then playfully slapped my butt as we walked up to him.

"She has a sister? Some people have all the luck," said Vince look of mock surprise on his face.

"Which room is the liveliest tonight at least as far as music?" Susa asked slipping the doorman a silver piece.

"The upper room has a Gnome group in with a real bard. They've already had to break open a fourth hogshead," he replied pocketing the silver and giving me an appraising look.

"A bit manly for your tastes isn't she?" Vince said, looking at my broad shoulders and overall muscular tone.

"Last time you accused me of not having any taste at all and said that I'd fuck anything that moves. Make up your mind, Vince," said Susa with a wink.

Vince laughed, bowed to acknowledge the touch, and then let us into the brothel itself.

We entered into a large foyer, which stretched up to the roof of the building. We were greeted once again, this time by a naked slave girl. "What are your ladyships' pleasures tonight?" She asked from a kneeling position. She was Human, about our age. Pretty and fit without being exaggerated about it.

"Music," said Susa. "I believe the upper room has what we desire."

"Of course, your ladyship, will you be requiring any extra company tonight that you would like to arrange for now?" replied the slave girl to Susa request.

"Not at this time no. Just lead on," said Susa.

With that the slave girl got up and another took her place at the door. As we walked up the stairs behind the slave, I couldn't help by watch the lovely curve of her bare buttocks and long legs. Idly I wondered what it would be like to be fucked by a skilled sex slave.

The female form is considered the height of both

physical beauty and perfection with the City of Gates. So all are expected to worship at its altar. That and the generally asexual nature of the dominant Elven cultural bias means that bisexuality among women, especially younger women, is not just normal but expected. A girl's first lover is usually her best friend, and this should start no later than 12 or 13. It's through this exploration that a girl gains a sense of both how her own body experiences pleasure and how to provide such pleasure to others.

I was a late bloomer. I didn't really start to have in interest in sex until just before I set out to find my own way in this world. My first lover had been my trainer (and still the ugliest woman I have ever known). Being that I was young without a copper to my name, I had traded sexual favours for that training. And yes I am well aware of the irony spreading my legs in an attempt to avoid spreading my legs like my mother.

Distracting myself from thoughts of sex, I asked Susa "Why the escort? I thought you knew where we were going?"

"I do, but the Queen walks a fine line between indulging their clients and privacy. By always traveling to your chosen destination with an escort they make sure that your stated intentions are your intentions," explained the little warlock.

Finally we came to a large set of double doors. As soon as they were opened loud and energetic music could be heard coming from the room behind. Inside were about a fifty people, all enraptured by the sound. Most were dancing on a large dance floor while the rest were either sitting in booths or standing on the edges swaying or clapping to the rhythm that the Gnomes were belting out.

We found a table and Susa was able to wave down a wench who soon came back with two flagons of very good mead and a small plate of sweet meats and cheese.

Both of us tore into the plate of food, and the mead

was quickly followed by a second, and we started to slow down a bit for the third, where we sat back and took in the music.

"This was a great choice, Susa," I said over the music. "I never would have expected this kind of audience in a whorehouse."

"Brothel," Susa corrected me. "A whorehouse is just about quick and dirty sex. A good brothel caters to much more varied entertainment, and it's neutral ground. Right now as we speak, merchants, Compacters, and anyone else with airs are debating politics, poetry, and philosophy in other rooms, and will continued to do so until well into the night. Sometimes they'll end the evening in a pleasure slave's arms, sometimes they'll have business agreements hammered out, and sometimes they'll have both. But officially what happens here stays here."

"And unofficially?" I asked cynically.

"Unofficially a surprising amount does stay behind closed doors. By Compact law a brothel owner can ban anyone from their property. That's very powerful encouragement to toe the line," she replied.

It was then that the serving wench came to our table and informed us that we had to settle our tab before we could order anything more. Unlike the girl who brought us here she was a free woman working for tips. Along with a tiny g-string the only other thing she 'wore' was a magically animated tattoo of naked serving girl flinging a tankard of ale into the open mouth of a dwarf across her shoulder blades.

I reached into my bag and pulled out two gold pieces and asked if we could start a tab.

"Of course," was her reply with a warm smile and a twinkle in her eye. She left making sure that I got a good look at both her ass and the moving ink as she did so.

"Hey I thought I was going to get this one? You got the last two places," said Susa.

"I got the bonus from Serett, let me pay," was my reply.

"You've already spent that bonus, Annie. Let me pick this one up." She said with a note of stubborn pride in her voice.

"No, I got this one," I said with equal stubbornness. "Tell you what; you can fill up the tab next time," I said.

"How about I drink you for it? Winner buys the night," she replied.

I looked at Susa and did drunk math in my head. She's barely over 5' tall and maybe weighs in at 100 pounds wet. And every spellcaster I've ever known couldn't hold their liquor. So no way a big strapping fighter like me could lose, right?

I smiled and said "you're on."

Now I'd like to remind you that this was drunk math, which was the reason I missed an important factor of the equation. Warlocks like Susa channel magical energy through their bodies, meaning that that they have an amazing tolerance for pain, the ability to withstand illness, and oh CAN DRINK DWARVES UNDER THE FUCKING TABLE.

But as I said, I had forgotten this which is why the rest of the night happened.

When the wench came back, Susa decided to up the stakes. "Do you have any Fey Brandy Wine left?"

"Yes but your tab is not enough to cover a glass," started the wench in reply

Before she could finish, Susa pulled out 10 more gold pieces and said, "Bring us two glasses."

The wench grabbed up the coins and ran back to the bar.

"Fey Brandy Wine, what's that?" I asked.

"A distilled wine from Faire: It's like nothing you've ever had before. One sip tastes different from the one before, and it will make you feel better about yourself and the world around you than you've ever felt before," Susa replied with a note of almost lust in her voice.

Well that got me curious, so when the serving girl returned with two wine glasses of what appeared to be water, I was not impressed. At least not until Susa took one, and flicked a black finger nail against the side of the glass. Then a wave of dark reds and blacks ripped away from the side of the glass; when they hit the other side they changed colour, and soon the glass was a swirling mass of colour so bright it actually glowed.

When I did the same, bright blues and reds started across the glass, but the end was the same.

"Okay, I'm impressed," I said.

"Now taste it," pressed Susa as she sipped from her glass.

As I took a sip I realized that I would never in all my life, taste something that gave me as much pleasure as what that Brandy Wine did. At least until I tried another sip, and then a third. I assume there was a fourth but till this day I can't remember it.

# Chapter Two

When I awoke next morning I was tired, very sore, and nursing one hell of a hangover. I was in a large soft bed and entangled with me was Susa. I barely recognized the fact that both of us we naked before the pressing need to throw up hit me.

Scrambling out of bed and into an adjacent room which praise the Gods was a bathroom. My need was so great that I barely registered that my right leg was caught on something, that it took a hard pull to partially free me, and that I was dragging a weight of some sort behind me.

The subsequent crash and cry of pain and surprise from Susa also didn't really register.

The bathroom was equipped with all the magical touches: self-heating bath, self-cleaning toilet, and a full sized reflective wall just to name a few. I managed to make it to the toilet in time and was retching there for a minute before I felt a pair of little hands pull back my hair. Sliding down to the floor I found that I lacked the energy to get up and decided that the floor was cool enough for me to lie on forever.

Susa had other ideas. She pulled me up to a sitting position and then got me to open my eyes.

When I was able to focus I saw that she was still naked but holding two cups before her.

"Drink this, you'll feel better," she shouted.

"Merciful gods, Susa, don't shout," I said in what I thought was a normal speaking voice. Turns out I was shouting even louder than Susa because we both winced when I spoke.

"I wasn't, I was whispering," she said an annoyed voice, still holding the cups.

"I get that," I whispered back and took one of the cups from her. It contained water and something else that I couldn't figure out but soon after I finished it I did start to feel better.

"Thanks, what was in that?" I asked.

"Water and neutralize poison powder. It will help you recover from the hangover faster. Now get up we both could use a very hot bath right about now," she said as she grabbed one arm, wrapped it around her neck, and started to pull me up. It was right about then, with Susa's head on my chest, that I looked into the mirror and registered what I actually saw there.

My hair was a mess, but that was to be expected given

the rather hard partying I had probably been doing. However it was now, along with my now perfectly trimmed eyebrows, a bright blood red colour. It was also the only hair on my body. As I've mentioned before, I wasn't as consistent about my personal care back then, and that certainly applied to the removal of body hair. But it appeared that I gotten the bug last night. I'd gone completely Elven: hairless arms, hairless legs, and bare pussy. This last one meant that I had no problem seeing the gold ring which now pierced my clit.

And that wasn't my only new piece of jewellery. A gold one inch ring was now mounted in each nipple along with a half inch ring through my left nostril with a chain that ran up to my left ear lobe. Hanging from the centre of the chain was a small tear drop ruby, the twin of the one that was mounted in my navel. As I stood there with my mouth open, I also realized that my tongue now sported a large stud as well.

But there was more; my lips and finger nails were as red as my hair. As were my nipples and my vulva lips, now that I could see past the gold rings. Looking down, sure enough, even my toe nails were the same blood red. Did I mention that I was also wearing an ankle chain off my right leg which ran to Susa's left leg? No, well, add that to the tally as well.

Of course the piece de resistance was my wild black and red eye make-up. Similar in style to Susa's but of a different execution than Susa's the make-up made me look like some sort of extreme angel of war.

Those were just the permanent shots to my dignity. Welts and bruises of various sizes criss-crossed my entire body, with a large proportion covering my breast and back area. They were fresh and some of them still welled with blood.

Somewhere during this self examination I screamed, which really didn't help my head or Susa's right at the moment. But it did help get the adrenaline rushing which in turned kicked all the remaining cobwebs out of my head.

Susa's brain must also have been on the uptake now, because she took one look at my face and said "I take it we are suffering from some memory problems about last night?"

I nodded vigorously which hurt like the hells so I said a quiet. "Yes."

Looking at the warlock I realized that Susa appeared to have the same body modifications done as I did. I mean I always knew her tits were black and pierced. She'd flashed them to anyone who'd look. But the other modifications; those were new to me. The welts and bruises across her body strangely eased my anxiety. Whatever happened last night we'd both been through it.

"Annie, when you let go, you really let go," she said with what sounded to me like approval.

"You let all of them happen to me?" I asked waving my hand at my body. I'm a little ashamed to admit it now but blaming Susa made me feel a lot better at the time.

"Now wait a minute; yes, I suggested the Fey Brandy Wine, but you drank it with fair warning of what you happen. And you agreed to the drinking contest. Granted that I didn't stop anything that was going on, but in my own defence I wasn't exactly sober either."

I groaned more from the growing horror of knowing that I was not going to like what I was going to hear about last night.

Susa got more water from the pitcher in the bath room and handed it to me. "Look we both are in desperate need to a bath. I'll explain everything once we're soaking."

The idea of a hot full body bath did sound really good right then. We stepped up into the bath which rapidly filled with water so hot that I thought we'd started to boil. The tub was large enough that we could sit opposite from each other and still have room for two more people.

As we soaked more of my body started report it. I surreptitious checked for any other surprises. I was pretty sure that along with fucking someone last night I'd had my first experience with anal sex. My first guess was the brunette across the bath, but she lacked the necessary equipment.

"How much do you remember about last night?" asked Susa when she saw me getting more restless.

I thought back and said finally "I remember the first sip of the Feywine and thinking how marvellous it tasted, how it kept changing flavour with ever sip. I remember the second and third sips and that's pretty much it."

Susa just nodded her head and then said, "Okay, I've heard that memory loss was a concern with Fey Brandy, but I never thought it would be so complete. The neutralize poison may help a bit with your memory but we're going to be here for a while."

"Alright, but first question, how did we end up like this?" I asked holding up the ankle chain.

"That was me being a bit paranoid. I wanted to make sure we stayed together just in case things got out of hand."

"Out of hand! How in the Nine Hells don't you call being stripped, shaved, dyed, pierced, beaten, and from what I can tell butt fucked at least once not getting out of hand?"

"No one died or was crippled. That was what I was mostly worried about. Annie you were impulsive and unpredictable last night. That's a dangerous combination when combined with your strength, not to mention your comfort with deadly violence. I was worried if you changed your mind at any point last night there may have been more blood spilt," said Susa with dead seriousness.

"Wait you're making it sound like you were more worried about me getting out of hand than someone getting out of hand with me?" I replied.

"Yes that's exactly what I meant," said Susa.

She then dunked her head to clean her hair. After Susa came up for air she started to tell the tail about last night in earnest.

"Alright we were three quarters of the way through the Fey Brandy Wine when a couple of guys I knew came up and joined us. Introductions were made, more food and wine was ordered, and the story of how we ended up in the bar that night was retold. When we got to the part about the duel, you got a bit animated in your tale telling. You picked up a couple of beef ribs you'd ordered and started to re-enact the duel. You were doing fine until you nailed a waitress with one of your backswings, spilling drinks including a large glass of red wine over yourself.

"I told the bartender that we'd pay for the drinks and that table's replacement round as means of apology. Turns out that table was enjoying your show at much as we were they offered to buy us the round.

"So there you were in Gwen's white dress, half covered in red wine. I made one little comment about the return of the Princess of Blood and you decided to take it as your new nickname, only changing it to the Blood Princess.

"That met with a hearty approval from the crowd, with toasts being made to the Blood Princess, which you accepted graciously. You were about to continue with your re-enactment of the duel when someone suggested that you should take off your dress before the stain set in. I guess you figured Gwen would be pissed if you returned the dress ruined, so off it came to be soaked. You then finished the duel dressed only in your thong."

Half way through the story I started to sink deeper into the water, when she got to the "only my thong part" my head was completely under I and didn't come back up until I ran out of air.

"Any of this ringing any bells?" she asked.

"No," I said in a weak voice.

"Ooookay. After you finished your re-enactment you

were toasted and accepted the applause from the crowd. You seemed to have been emboldened by the attention because next then I knew I had your tongue down my throat in one of the most passionate kisses I've had for a while. Turning to the crowd, you stated that you were using your royal prerogative as a princess to fuck any commoner you wanted; starting with me. At which point you ripped my dress off, threw me over your shoulder, and set off to get a room."

I looked at Susa, horrified that I would say and done such a thing no matter what state I was in. "Oh gods Susa I'm so sorry I would never have done something…" My ranting apology was cut off as a bolt of magical energy went past my head and blew out the window behind me.

"Annie, do you for one second believe that if it wasn't consensual on my part we would be here in the tub right now?" said Susa with a hard look in her eye.

I nodded my head in agreement. I always have to remind myself that Susa is deadly with her spells. I've seen others try and take advantage of her because she was tiny, most of them are dead.

"It was nice being handled instead of handling for a change, so I decided to play the bottom for the night. Besides, you'd let the reins go. I was curious to see where the night would go," she continued.

"So where were we? Right, me over your shoulder. With your conquest in hand, you went up to the Mistress of the house and demanded their best suite and paid their nightly rate for their best worker without taking her with us."

Susa smiled very sweetly at me. "That was the nicest compliment anyone has paid me in a long time by the way."

I suddenly felt the urge to sink below the water again. Drowning wasn't a bad way to die, and I'm sure the Queen of Death would appreciate the reasoning.

"Anyways, somewhere between the stairs and room we lost what remained of our clothing. To be honest I can't remember that how exactly happened but we entered here completely naked and you threw me onto the bed laid on top of me and started to kiss and lick my nipples. Then you became fixated by my piercings. You were instantly enamoured by them and asked me where you could get the same done.

"Well, when I told you that this brothel does all sorts of body art you grabbed my wrist and ran down the stairs to the bar again demanding to see the tattooist."

"Were we...both still...?"I started to ask hesitantly.

"Naked? Oh yes, and fully aroused as well. When was the last time you had sex that you actually wanted and enjoyed? Cause Gods you were in heat last night.

"Everyone was stunned by this new performance so no one really said anything. The evening mistress knew we were good for the money so she agreed to put things on a tab. She directed us to the body artist studio, and got the guy up.

"Turns out the artist was a Dwarf who was already awake from all the cheering and screaming around "the Blood Princess" so he was more than happy to push pieces of metal through you.

"Now this guy was the flamingest gay Dwarf I have ever met. He took one look at you and said 'This, this is the Blood Princess! No no no, we shall have to do better for someone of that name.'

"So for the next two hours and a bottle of brandy wine you had the makeover that your sisters and I have been trying get give you for months," Susa said gleefully.

He started talking ideas about looks and makeup but you pointed at me and said, "I want to look just like her...

"...only in blood red," I finished, not sure where that line came from, but knowing it was true.

"You're remembering that's great," said Susa pleased

with a pleased voice.

Well first step was an alchemical bath to remove your body hair, which you thought was great because of how your Elven half-sisters never have to shave their legs,"

"Wait I said that?"

Susa nodded her head in the affirmative. "At least you thought it was great until the bath started to burn and they wouldn't let you leave the bath. That was one of those danger points I mentioned earlier, until the Dwarf said something about how he'd heard less complaining from a compact tween. That calmed you down right quick and you sulked through the rest of the treatment."

I frowned at what Susa was saying. I've dealt with injuries and pain before a little skin irritation shouldn't bother me. But neither did kissing Susa and ripping her cloths off in front of two dozen strangers.

"How long until the hair grows back?" I asked. I hadn't heard of this treatment before but figured it was better than the pumice stone that I currently used.

Now it was Susa's turn to look puzzled. "Uhmm never. The treatment was alchemical. It destroyed the hairs at their roots. That's pretty standard for most women."

"You mean… The Elven look is permanent."

"Yes. Why the concern? I was surprised that you hadn't gone that way already. Your mother worked in a tavern; I would have thought that she would have had you done years ago. I mean most Compact girls go Elven as soon as the hair starts to grow," Susa said.

"My mother wanted me to, but I always thought she was getting me ready to join her trade," I said. It was strange I'd never shared that with anyone before, and when I did I had suddenly felt better for some reason.

Susa eye's widened for a second and I saw her mind click over.

"Wait, you mean that all this time you've been afraid of ending up like your mother? Oh gods no wonder… Let me guess, that slug of trainer has been the only one you've been fucking on a regular basis and that's been for rent, right?" she asked with surprising gentleness.

I nodded yes.

"Oh Annie, if we'd known sooner. I'm surprised Gwen never said anything. Maybe she was too scared to because she didn't want to risk losing you," she said.

I could tell that mind of hers was working a mile a minute.

"What? Who didn't say anything," I asked.

"Gwen; Annie to anyone who knows what to look for, you are so out of sync that it's quite frankly dangerous. Your mind and your body are really out of balance. I think that's the reason why you're so skilled in battle. It's the only time you listen to your body.

Now my anger was rising, but not at Susa; it was just rising.

"Can we get back to what happened last night and out of my head please?" I asked hotly.

Never let be said that Susa could not recognize dangerous ground when she saw it.

"After the body hair got axed, the Dwarf started with the dye, hairstyle, and makeup. The dwarf used alchemical dyes and did the job pretty quickly; he was inspired by my less than usual body colour so along with your lips and nails he also did your nipples and pussy lips."

"Why didn't you stop him," I all but screamed at her.

"At the time you kept insisting that you wanted to look just like me only blood red. You were very clear on that fact. I didn't know any of it was permanent till they were pretty much done. I thought it was all reversible and at worst you have to live with the dye job because of one drunken night."

"But you had it done," I said accusingly as I pointed to her black nipples.

Susa's eyes turned hard. "When this was being done to

me, it was by a devil while my mind had been taken by a Succubus to be trained in one night, real time, as a warlock. You know that dream time works differently than real time? That one night for me was six months of rigid training with sexual discipline, by a creature CREATED to know everything about how to use sex as an inducement."

I looked at Susa with stunned horror. That was the first time I had heard Susa's story. I had gotten hints from Gwen that Susa's becoming a warlock experience had been traumatic, but I'd never gotten the details till then. Gods, first slavery, and then the offer of the coven, sexual slavery and torture in the guise of magical training, and after, she *still* had the resolve to rescue people, for her, the passage of six months: It wasn't surprising that Susa seemed insane at times.

It also explained her level of determination to get something done when her mind was set to it.

"Sorry." I said and left a difficult silence between us for a minute. Turning towards the mirror I realized that I liked the red and black makeup. Sure, it was loud, sure it didn't look like something that someone named Annie, but it did really look like someone called the Blood Princess. I also realized that I must have had one hell of a great hair style to go with it and that I couldn't remember it.

"I sorry I can't remember the hairdo. It must have been really something," I said with a sorrowful voice.

"Well, that we can change," said Susa. "Here stand up."

I stood up and Susa turned me so that we both faced the mirrored wall.

"Now flick your hair like this," said the warlock. She then flicked her hair forward and back causing her equally long hair to do the same.

She then staggered a bit, and had to hold onto me to keep her balance.

"Okay not the best thing to do mid hangover," she

said.

But I really didn't notice because not only was her hair completely dry, but it was beautifully cut and styled as if she had just walked out of a salon.

Realizing what that implied, I did the same, and while it didn't do anything good for my hangover I looked at my own shoulder length curly hair cut and teased hairdo.

Okay now that was cool.

"Is this permanent too?" I asked.

"Until you want to change the style. It will even shorten your hair," replied Susa with girlish glee. "Then you're going to have to have the ritual recast. But until then say good bye to bed head, helmet head, and bad hair days."

Turning to me she said "I've never had the cash to get it done myself before last night, but since you were having it done I'd might as well too."

No more helmet hair? Even with my anti beauty stand, this is big issues. Oh hells yes! Okay last night wasn't a complete loss.

Looking at my mirror image once again I noticed the welts and bruises again and I wanted to know the rest of the story for last night.

"What about the welts and bruises?" I asked.

"That all came about because of the piercings," said Susa as she sat back down into the steaming water.

"After they finished with your hair they started on the body mods. Now I'm not sure if it was because of the alchemical bath, or the attention or what but you were becoming increasingly aroused through the night."

When Susa mentioned this, my entire body started to tingle as if every nerve in my skin started to fire at once. And even though there were immersed in hot water I felt my nipples start to harden.

"I think you were still a bit stung by the earlier Compact Tween comment because you decided to get the piercings done without the local pain killers.

"The ears, nostril and navel were fine. The tongue was where you started to make little what sounded like sexual noises instead of gasps of pain. When the Dwarf started on your nipples it was clear that you were finding everything more a turn on then painful.

"Once he was done with the nipple rings there was only the clit ring left. And there this presented a problem. Even aroused it wasn't big enough to get properly ringed, so the dwarf asked if you wanted it through the sheath instead. You insisted the clit itself, so he trimmed back the sheath a bit. This combination of pain and fingering got you going again, and when he did finally drive the needle through you came very loudly," Susa said.

I missed that last part of what my friend was saying. As she had mentioned each body part being pierced I felt a sudden sharp pain their as if I was reliving the event. My arousal was also increasing. I started to find it difficult to breathe and I found that I was sweating even more than before. When she started to feel talk about my clit I started to feel the light headed and then I climaxed.

# Chapter Three

Only I wasn't in the bath anymore I was on a padded chair, still naked with my legs spread open and a browned haired Dwarf standing between them. The dwarf had one hand upon my groin holding that part of my body down. I couldn't see where his other hand was but a part of me did feel the strange sensation of cold metal sliding through my clitoris.

I said a small part because the rest of body was rigid and climaxing from one of the most powerful orgasms I have ever felt.

"Well we have quite the untamed filly here," said the Dwarf.

"She gives a pretty show that's for sure. Half the crowd just came with her," said another voice that I did not recognize.

As I came down from the rush, I looked up and saw about twenty people above me. Most appeared to either have just finished jacking off or had someone assisting them to do so.

Seeing what I had made the mixed crowd of men and woman do; I felt another surge of sexual energy. *I* had made them do that: I had made them so aroused that they creamed their breeches. There was a power there, a power that I had felt before in a pit fight when I had made a crowd roar with blood lust. It was a heady rush that I wanted more of.

It was also then that I realized that should not have been feeling what I was feeling. Where was the embarrassment, the humiliation? I was having the strangest feeling of being in a body but it wasn't mine.

Calming down, I almost felt like the thinking part of my mind needed to catch up to my where my emotions and bodily sensations were.

And right then my bodily sensations were telling me that I really wanted to check out my new piece of jewellery.

"Can I see it?" I heard myself asking the Dwarf.

"Just lay back for a bit more Blood Princess I just want to get some healing salve on the region so that it heals clean," was his reply.

I leaned back in frustration and decided to centre my breathing instead. It was then that I realized that I was holding onto someone's hand.

Turning I say a naked Susa still holding onto my hand,

a mixture of lust and surprise on her face.

"Welcome back Annie," she said with a smile brushing back a stray hair from my face. "You have any more surprises for me tonight? 'Cause if you tell me you're the female aspect of Storm Lord right now I'd believe you,"

I didn't answer her; instead, I flexed my arm and pulled her towards me. She rose up and without even asking continued to move until her lips locked with mine.

There was a chorus of ooos and ahh from the crowd above us from the perceived romantic moment they were seeing.

I broke the kiss when I felt the dwarf hitting my thigh.

"Alright now you're ready. Stand up and let's get a look at the Blood Princess," he said.

Breaking the kiss I got up and turned to where the walled mirror was.

Like I had before, I had the feeling that I was looking at a complete stranger. Before me was one of the warrior amazons of bardic tales. The black and red makeup along with the savage cut and colour of the hair made this creature look dangerous. A sneer appeared on her face and for the first time that I could ever remember someone looked more intimidating that Susa when she went off on a tear.

The biggest difference the second time around my detached self noted was that instead of embarrassment or shock with the image I felt… well I loved the effect.

"The Blood Princess. It's not a joke anymore. She really exists," Susa whispered next to me.

Looking at my friend's reflection I saw a completely new expression on her face. A faraway look, as if she was staring at something a great distance into the future. Mixed with that was a look of awe.

"And my first Black Bitch," I said giving Susa a check with my hip.

Susa looked up at me startled. "What did you say?" she asked.

"Just something that popped into my head. The Blood Princess and her Black Bitches. I think it would work as a group name, don't you? It's memorable at least," I replied.

"Oooo I like it, I know just what I can do for the armour. I've always wanted to do something in leather armour that was both functional and fashionable," said the Dwarf.

I turned to the dwarf. "Really?" I asked.

"It's a Dwarf thing dearie don't get worked up about it."

"Gwen might have something to say about the name," said Susa with a bemused tone.

I was about to answer when a shrill cry rose up from the crowd.

"What is going on here?" said a woman who pushed through the crowd to stare down to where Susa and I were. She was a tall statuesque blonde that looked like a schoolboy's wet dream of his nanny. Big breasts, narrow waist, and wide hips; all kept in with a corset, short skirt and thigh high boots (black leather, of course. I mean what else would she be wearing).

I guessed she was one of the free women who worked in the brothel. Like many of those, she attempted to look young, but her definition of beauty was off. The result was that, while she had clear blemish free skin, it was stretched a little too tight over her face. Giving her a pinched bird like appearance.

Behind her was naked Half-Orc. Close to 6'6" in height her muscular body was covered with ritual scars and tattoos, her body jewellery was bone and ivory. She was an urban bard's stereotypical barbarian down to the bone through her nose. The large and spiked collar and heavy chain leash in the hands of the blonde did nothing to reduce her dangerous air.

"People are watching a real pain slut genuinely getting off, Debra," replied Susa with mocking tone.

"You," replied Debra with icy stare narrowing on my friend.

"I take it you know each other?" I whispered to Susa.

"Oh Debra claims to be the Queen's best domme and can make anyone her bitch," replied Susa.

"I take it you disagree?" I asked.

"Let's just say I've criticized some of her techniques and wonder openly why she always uses slaves in her public shows and leave it at that," Susa said.

"I can hear you! You cow!" said Debra, her anger visibly rising.

"Sit down Debra and enjoy the show. The Blood Princess is a refreshing change of pace," said an older man in the crowd. He was half dressed and a naked slave knelt between his legs as he talked.

"Why would I eat millet when there is steak," replied Debra scornfully. She then turned her eyes fully on me for the first time, giving me a look which I assumed was meant to make me run away in tears.

I giggled. I mean seriously earlier tonight I'd killed a Hobgoblin champion in a duel. I'd survived pit fight against Humans and Orcs twice my weight. Now I was supposed to be intimidated by an over magiced brothel dominant?

She was just so…cute.

To make matter worst it was a contagious giggle. Susa caught it almost immediately, and then the dwarf and his attendants started then the crowd. Even the Half-Orc showed a ghost of a smile.

That was enough for Debra, she literally jumped down into the Dwarf's work area stalked over to me and slapped me, across the face.

"You need to discipline your pet in the face of her betters Susa," she said to the warlock.

It wasn't a hard slap, but it was painful. She knew something about pain that was for sure. Not that I cared. It got me angry more than anything else. I pulled back my arm ready to clock her when I felt this heavy weight upon it. Turning I saw that Susa had literally wrapped her entire upper body around my arm and was using all 100 of her pounds to keep it in place.

"We accept the challenge. What stakes?" said Susa in a hurried voice.

"Banishment from the Queen," replied Debra. "I'll not have you attempt to take away my clients through novelty only to leave them with an inferior product."

It was then that I finally got it.

"She thinks that you're trying to horn in on her business?" I asked Susa.

Susa just nodded in the positive. Her eyes didn't leave the blonde dominatrix.

"I have a counter Debra. If Annie wins you not only leave the Queen but the City of Gates as well," said Susa with a lilt in her voice that came when she was infusing her words with magic.

"And if I win?" Debra asked.

"I'll be your bottom for a year," replied Susa.

For the first time I saw Debra smile and not surprisingly there wasn't any warmth to it what so ever.

"Agreed," she replied.

"A bargain has been made who here will witness it?" Debra asked the crowd.

"We all will," shouted the older man who spoke before.

"Especially if they duel now," cried a second voice from the back.

The crowd roared with approval with that remark. Before she replied Susa pulled me back a bit then looked me straight in the eye. "You're high as a pixie's voice aren't you?" she asked.

"What?" I heard myself say.

Susa took a deep breath and then said to me, "Annie, I've just agreed to have you doing something, but you're not entirely you right now. You can back out now, if you so choose. But if you stay in and win it will get rid of cruel bitch that's responsible for physically and emotionally crippling several dozen slaves."

I felt myself smile down at Susa, seeing for the first time honest conflict in her eyes. I couldn't resist. I leaned forward and kissed her hard on the mouth.

"You cute when you're scared," I told her. I then looked up and assessed the Half-Orc. As I had noted before she had a very savage appearance. But looking closer I saw that like Debra's beauty, it was manufactured and artificial. Granted she looked tough and strong but all Half-Orcs look tough and strong. But her body language didn't speak well for someone who was used to violence. Despite the bone and scars, I doubted Sofia had ever been out of the city. I figured that I could take her in any physical contest.

"I can take her, especially if the stakes are high," I said to Susa.

"Okay, but the least I can do it share it with you," was her reply. Turning to Debra, Susa smiled dangerously and said. "Agreed."

Before the blonde could say anything, Susa spoke to the gathering crowd. "However, I believe since we have an audience who appears to have a growing interest in this duel, that we should leave it up to them the nature of the contest," she said aloud.

"No, this is between the two us," said Debra harshly.

"Oh come now Debra, the Blood Princess has gotten all made up would you deny us the pleasure of her performance?" said the older man again. The slave seemed to have finished her job and closed up his breeches. Now in fully clothed he had a much stronger air of command.

"Of course Master Astor, just given how late the hour

I'd thought that everyone would have had more pressing things to do," replied Debra smoothly.

"And miss something as unique as this? What says everyone?" asked Aster to the crowd.

The crowd, that now numbered several dozen, roared their willingness to watch.

"So what should the contest involve?" asked Astor. It was amazing; in a matter of seconds Astor had seized control of the situation from Debra and now was fully in charge.

"The wrack," shouted someone.

"Wild pony," shouted another.

"Water wheel," called out a third.

"I say the Lord Astor should decide," sounded out a fourth.

The crowd's blood was up that was for sure. Once again they roared their approval.

Lord Astor put up his hands in mock surrender. "Very well! Once again I will accept the heavy burden of leadership," he said with all seriousness.

The crowd started to laugh even harder.

Once again Astor put up a hand and the crowd settled down.

"We have two fine fillies here. We should test them appropriately. Prepare them as ponies and let's see who breaks first on the millstones.

Once again the crowd roared its approval.

"To the millstones!" shouted the crowd.

"Mill-stones! Mill-stones! Mill-stones!" chanted the crowd.

Once again Susa grabbed my hand and turned so that she looked me in the eye. "Whatever happens over the next few minutes do not resist! They're going to talk tough but you're not in any real danger understand?" said Susa to me quickly.

I nodded in understanding though in fact I really didn't

at first. Then I saw several crowd members leap down into the makeover area. They wore Dark Queen's livery and they were obvious bouncers meant to keep the crowd in line.

With suitable reverence they assisted Lord Astor down onto the floor. He strove forward to where Debra, and Susa, who from somewhere found a shift to put on, now stood.

It was the first time that I got a good look at Lord Astor. He was smaller than I first thought. When he was talking I thought he was six feet or more. Close up, though, I could see that he was no taller than me. He did have a powerful build, however, and a natural air of command. It was then that I remembered that House Astor was one of the Compact families and I swallowed. That meant that this stocky bald man was the closest thing the City of Gates had to royalty.

"Ladies with the crowd's approval I am now to officiate this contest. Please tell your slaves that they need to follow my orders," Lord Astor said smoothly.

Debra didn't say a word but just handed the leash over to Astor. Then Sofia grunted in acknowledgement.

"The Blood Princess is not mine or anyone else's slave, but she does recognise your authority in this and only this circumstance my lord," replied Susa.

Lord Astor tilted his head first to Susa and then to me. Then he spoke, "while I acknowledge the statement, I cannot allow any perceived differences in how either is treated to affect neither the outcome nor any wagers that are being made at this time."

Astor nodded to one of the Queen's bouncer, a large well-built north man well over six feet in height.

The blond giant came up to me producing a length of silk rope from one of his pouches.

"Hands behind your back Blood Princess," he said in an amazingly quiet voice.

I looked over to Susa who gave me another reassuring

smile.

I did as requested.

With practiced ease he tied my hands behind my back. Then as if it was the most natural thing to do, the stage hand ran his fingers over my groin and rear. While it doesn't say much for my honed fighter reflexes I have to admit that I was so taken aback by the brazen violation that my only reaction was a cry of surprise when his fingers quickly entered and then exited both my pussy and my anus.

"Tight and wet, the way a good fuckbitch should be," he commented to his fellows.

The bouncer then produced a choke chain from another pouch. He threw the chain around my neck and cinched it tight, leaving the end dangling between my breasts. Finally he pulled out a leather leash and attached it to dangling end of the choke chain. Once again taking the opportunity to give my right breast a hard squeeze and pulled its nipple ring hard enough to cause the newly healed holes to bleed again.

This time however I was ready.

Without even looking I stomped down with my right heel, driving it hard into the top of one of the bouncer's feet.

I felt and heard at least two bones in his foot break and smiled as he let out a bellow of genuine pain and collapsed onto the floor.

The bouncer's scream of pain and fall got everyone's attention. Lord Astor and the other bouncers were shocked when it hit them that the supposedly helpless girl had just dropped one of the Dark Queen's toughest bouncers in one shot.

"As I said Lord Astor the Blood Princess is a free woman with every right to defend her person against the actions of others," said Susa quickly and smoothly.

Then without missing a beat, she leaned down and

retrieved the end of the leash from the still moaning man's hand. Turning to me she pressed the chain to my lips.

"Kiss the leash like you mean it," she said in a surprising commanding whisper.

"What? Why should I do that?" I asked back in an equally quiet whisper.

"These people are used to dealing with slaves and submissives. They don't know how to deal with someone who can legally fight back. By kissing your leash you're publicly showing that you will submit. Everyone else will understand the rules on how to treat you better."

All of this didn't really make sense to me but I'd promised Susa that I'd go through with this contest so I leaned down and kissed the leash like a fresh lover. Susa then took the leash over to Lord Astor.

Lord Astor accepted the leash with a solemn expression, recognizing his role in the performance.

"Good now we shall proceed," he said, turning to leave.

Walking out of the room I fell in behind Lord Astor right next to the Sofia. She was big that's for sure, towering more than foot above me and every inch of it muscle. But she moved like I expected, slow and ponderous without and any real grace.

We walked for about five minutes through a number of corridors until we stepped out onto what appeared to be an open air theatre. Where the stage for the theatre should have been there were two large millstones. Each stone was equipped with an eight foot rail which would turn the stone around a grooved pedestal. The rail was about four inches thick and was worn very smooth with use. Along the handle were three yokes for an animal to be tied on to provide the power to turn the grind stone.

Despite being the middle of the night, magical lighting along the front of stage made it appear as bright as day. We also had a pretty good view of the theatre seating and I was surprised to see that half of its fifty or so seats were already filled. With more people, in various stages of dress, taking up the remaining seats as we came into view. The seats themselves were interesting. There were individual chairs instead of benches, each row was spaces about five feet apart and rose at a very sharp angle. This allowed for plenty of room for the various attendants, partners and sex slaves who were also arriving to see to the needs of the guests. In total there must have been close to two hundred people there to watch the show.

I should have been embarrassed, I should have felt humiliated. I was naked, bound and being lead around on a leash in front of hundreds of people. And I was about to take part in some sort of sexual contest. And I only felt ... excited! That and truth be told more than a little turned on.

"Alright, these two ponies need to be prepared," said Astor.

As if by magic several stage hands appeared carrying harnesses and other tack.

Sofia and I were then oiled down so that our bodies glistened in the light, and every muscle group could be plainly seen. No body part no matter how intimate was missed. However there was no poking around this time so I kept my feet to myself.

While this was going on our hair was drawn back into pony tails. And a Human woman was doing a colour comparison of our hair with a set of what looked to me were fly swatters. You know the kind about a foot and half long tail of horse hair with an eight inch long handle about an inch and a half across.

Once the oiling was done, we were next fitted with our shoes. It was then that I really started to get the idea of how serious this 'contest' was going to get. Glancing at them they looked like six inch spiked heels. It was only when I saw them being put on Sofia that I realized that the needle sharp 'spike' was inverted and pointed directly at her heel.

If she relaxed off of the ball of her foot at all she'd skewer her entire foot.

"These are pony trainers. Don't put your foot down or you'll go lame, and we'll have to put you down," said one of the stage hands to me as I was fitted with my own set of shoes. They went on easy enough to get on, like a pair of flip flop sandals. But that ease was part of the 'training'.

Once they were on I was told to walk around. I usually fight on the balls of my feet and generally consider myself pretty light footed. But walking with my heels six inches off the ground with no support was a whole new challenge.

For the first time that night I shot Susa a 'what in the Nine Hells have you gotten me into' look.

She gave me a reassuring smile. Then turned to Astor and played her trump card.

"Lord Astor do you truly thing that a free woman can compete against a disciplined and, at least according to Debra, fully trained sex slave?"

"The Blood Princess agreed to the contest warlock, fairness is no longer a matter of concern," sneered Debra. Too late did the blonde haired pro-domme realize that she had just interrupted Lord Astor.

"You're not trying to back out of the contest are you?" he asked suspiciously, icily ignoring Debra.

"Oh no, my lord, I'm just asking a hypothetical question," replied Susa in an even voice.

"Hypothetically speaking, then no I'd say that all other things being equal it would not be a fair contest," said Lord Astor, with genuine curiosity as to where Susa was going with this line of questioning.

"Then I propose in the interest of a fair and therefore more entertaining contest that Debra and I are also harnessed next to our slaves."

I could tell Susa was once again kicking magic into her words again because Lord Astor, the stage crew, Sofia and Debra all fell silent and stared at her. I was starting to get the impression that these people were not used to dealing with adventuring types like Susa and me. Certainly they did not appear to handle our straight out of the Elemental Chaos approach to life.

This reaction seemed to be infectious because soon the sudden lack of action caused members of the audience who were watching the prep show to take notice as well. Soon everyone in the theatre stopped talking.

Lord Astor started to laugh. There were good acoustics off of the stage as, the man's laughter filled the room with.

"And how would that make things more fair?" he asked Susa once he was in control of himself again.

"You are well aware of my rumours about me Lord Astor. That I was trained by a Succubus not only the arts of magic but other 'arts' as well: Arts, closer to the nature of a Succubus than magic. This training I feel makes me close to Sofia in competence, and therefore balances her. While Debra, as a dominatrix, is closer to the Blood Princess. Her experience balancing out my friend's enthusiasm," said Susa in a straight forward and logical manner.

"Are you insane? The wager has been made, the contest set, you can't change things now!" said Debra with genuine outrage.

"I can't; but Lord Astor can. We agreed to his adjudication," replied Susa calmly. Turing her attention back to Lord Astor, Susa continued "My Lord Astor, which would provide the crowd with the most entertainment: two ponies, or two sets of ponies?"

Lord Astor let a dramatic pause pass before he continued.

"Very well, in the interest of the crowd's entertainment, it shall be two sets of ponies," he said, signalling the four stage handlers to come forward.

"Gentlemen please prepare the two tops as ponies for the stones," he said to them.

Both Susa and Debra were then quickly stripped and

brought up to the same level of preparation as Sofia and I were. It was interesting to watch, the patterns of preparation was identical to what I had just endured. As if the preparation itself was part of the show.

Susa took the oiling and shoeing with good grace which seemed to garner approval from the stage hands. Debra on the other hand was letting things happen but let everyone know that she felt that she was beneath all this.

While I waited for the two new ponies to be readied, I took an opportunity to size up the new contestants.

I knew Susa was tough and stubborn. And though she was in possession of genuinely soft curves she was still very fit. Her biggest problem in this upcoming contest was simply a lack of physical strength. Heart and will she had a plenty, but raw muscle? Sorry no.

Debra's naked form continued to remind me some of the fey paintings I've seen; over worked, and too perfect. The edges and line of her hips and breasts, the perfection of her complexion, not to mention the sculpture of her abs, were just not possible on a natural Human. Hells they would have been hard to believe on an Elf. I guess she would have been attractive to some. To me though, Debra was too artificial to be truly beautiful. But artificial her muscles may be, they were still muscles with some strength to them.

And that was about the limit of my philosophizing at the time. All four of us were at the same point of preparation now. So the ritual could be continued at its proper pace.

Padded leather cuffs were now tied tightly to our wrists. Several links of chain were attached to each of them making it clear they were going too attached to something else. A complicated looking head harness and bridle set was strapped on. The harness had blinders which cut off our peripheral vision. I was surprised as to just how uncomfortable I felt with those blinders on. I guess it was due to my reliance on those angles in a fight.

The bit was a rather interesting contraption. It had a thick leather flange attached to one side that fitted in our mouths. If the bit's reins were slack the flange rested on my tongue effectively making it impossible for us to speak. However I it did not limit the volume of any other vocalizations, read screaming, that we cared to make. If the reins were tightened the flange drove painfully into our upper palate. If I turned my head to much the flange hit either one of my cheeks. Finally the contraption cut enough air off that it made breathing through your mouth of little use. I realized that soon all four of us were going to snorting through our noses just like real horses.

Once our 'tack' was added, we were lead to our harnesses. During our preparation one of the yokes had been removed leaving only two rigs on the millstone's arms. Sofia and I were bent over and attached on the inside harnesses, while Debra and Susa were positioned on the outside. The inside and outside ponies were then joined together via an ankle chain.

The actual position wasn't as bad as I was expecting. We were underneath the rail and our neck and shoulders rested on its back. This allowed for the main power of our shoulders and legs to push the millstone forward. The bridle reins were tied to the yoke and as long as I kept my head next up the flange stayed down on my tongue.

"Okay, are we ready to begin?" I thought. But it turned out there were two other additions to our getup.

The first was the 'fly swatter' which matched our hair colour. Turns out those were actually our tails. I grunted with surprise, as I then felt and a stage manager stand right behind me and start to rub his semi hard cock at first against my wet pussy lips. When it reached a certainly rigidity he unceremoniously shoved his cock hard into my cunt.

Not expecting to be fucked, I reflectively pulled away

from the invading member. This response got me a hard slap across my butt cheek.

"Now now, you fuck back like a good little pony," I heard the manager say.

Seeing as it did not have any real alternative I did as commanded.

After a minute I was close to my breaking point and cried out in misery when the stage manager fully pulled out.

"Oh this one not only tight but ready to pop," he said to his companions.

"This one as well," said the manger worked on Susa.

I had heard her groaning in frustration as well when he had pulled out.

The other attendants were commenting as well, but I didn't manage to hear them because my attention became focused once again as I felt the manger's cock head press against me. Only this time it was forcing its way past my sphincter and deep up my ass.

This was the first time I'd had anal sex and I found it a painful but not whole unpleasurable experience. As the attendant thrust into me I felt his cock slide hard past the back of my G spot. This was enough stimulation to cause it to react. Without being told I fucked back wanting him deeper and harder in me to increase that stimulation.

"There's a good pony. That right fuck me back," I heard the manager say.

After what seemed like hours, suddenly felt attendant's cock leave me completely "Right that should have nicely gapped you," said he.

My asshole did feel strange as the cool air tickled my insides in a way that it never had before.

That sensation only lasted for seconds however as my tail was inserted deep up my ass.

"Don't worry pony it's deep enough that it's not going to work out," said one of the stage hands noting my discomfort. "You think that feels good just wait till phoenix feathers start tickling your pussy."

I honestly didn't know what he was talking about but I didn't have long to wait to find out. Two long feathers were strapped to our thighs. The tips of these feathers reached up and brushed against our vaginas. Even moving I felt an itching sensation go through my groin that while not painful did cause things to heat up and swell even more.

Finally all four of us were ready. Astor now holding a long bull whip along with three other 'drivers', addressed both the ponies and the crowd.

"Alright the contest ends when one set of ponies can no longer turn their stone for an out loud count of ten spoken by myself.

"As usual a good pace is expected, and we have four drivers to make sure it is kept. Remember that all bets must be honoured before you leave the theatre. Is everyone ready to begin?" asked Astor.

I couldn't see the crowd, but it sounded like it was a hundred or more people shouted its affirmative.

I then heard several swishing sounds, and then the unmistakeable sound of leather against flesh. I felt burning on my upper thighs and reflectively started to move forward on the balls of my feet.

# Chapter 4

How long Susa and I turned that wheel I don't know. As I suspected my friend had the physical endurance to see herself though the task, but completely lacked the physical strength to offer any help. At best she was able to keep moving and did not make things harder for me.

But that was enough for me to still have the confidence of win. You see, my pit fighting trainer had used similar, though nowhere near as complicated, exercises for my strength and endurance training. It is best to just put your head down, look at the ground before you and move forward one step at a time. And no matter what just keep moving forward that one step. To stop for any reason was to invite disaster.

My trainer had even used a whip as a motivation technique, though she was nowhere as skilled with the damned thing as Lord Astor and the others were. They seemed to take great pleasure calling out a specific body part and then nailing it with the whip's tip.

"Right nipple," smack!

"Inner left thigh," crack!

"Clit ring," oh holy hells! Even Susa screamed when they nailed that one.

After five minutes of this it became clear that this was not going to be a quick contest. In order to preserve their own strength, the drivers settled into pattern of flogging up our backs and down our fronts.

In doing so, I was able to use that pattern to keep up the pace, ride through the cramps in my calves as the balls of my feet drove my entire body forward. I didn't allow the burning pain of the whipping to interrupt my pacing even when I screamed loudly when this hit my newly pierced nipples. Hells I was even able to handle how difficult my 'tail' made walking.

What I couldn't handle were the damned phoenix feathers brushing against my pussy lips. Their constant brushing down there had started out as an irritant. But soon, my lips swelled and as they did so did my arousal. It didn't take long before I was leaking pussy juice and, praying to every god that I knew to just free my hands for five seconds so that I could climax.

Not for the first time in my life the gods ignored my request, and I was left with sweaty palms which had slipped more than once from the rail. The desire within me caused my entire body to shake.

It was then that disaster struck; one of my knees buckled. I slipped badly enough that I drove the spike of the pony shoe deep into my heel, and lost my grip on the rail. This in turned jerked my head forward and drove the flange hard enough to the top of my mouth that I tasted blood. For several critical seconds, all that kept me from collapsing was my wrist cuffs.

"Looks as if the Blood Princess is finished," I heard someone say.

"Yeah she's leaking like a sieve. Even the first one in that pussy going to feel like sloppy seconds," said a second.

"I've always planned on removing the tail first. Her rear hole will be nicely gaped, but still tight. Perfect for a hard fuck," I heard a third say.

"One. Two. Three…" I heard Lord Astor count.

We'd completely stopped and I thought I heard Susa screaming at me through the bit to get up.

"Don't worry about it, Susa, you look about as ready for a good fuck as the Princess is," I heard someone say.

"…Four! Five!" continued Astor.

Then an image flashed in my mind. I recalled that blood haired beauty in the mirror. How confident she looked, how dangerous she appeared. There was someone who could move mountains. That image was the Blood Princess, and that was me. These bastards weren't laughing at the Annie that could be tolerated. They were laughing at the Blood Princess. And people did that at their peril.

And that's the first time that the Blood Princess actually came out to play.

With a sharp move of my shoulders I re-gripped the rail. I raised my head and after moving the all the fluids to the front of my mouth horked out a large ball of blood from my mouth.

Once more able to breathe I started to move the mill-stone again, this time at a greater pace than before. I must have caught Susa off guard, because I heard her squeal in surprise and I got the distinct impression that she was now running to keep up with me and the rail.

"Well it look as if we've been too soft on the ponies. If the Princess can set such a pace than Sofia and Debra can as well," I heard Lord Astor say to the other drivers.

After that the whip strike came even faster and with more strength.

But strangely I didn't care. My arousal was just as high and the burning in my loins if anything grew more intense, but as it did I found that I other pains my body felt lessened. It was more stimulation and I soon reached the point where my body was just stimulated as far as it would go. How long we went at that pace I don't know. The next intrusion to my pace was once again talk among the drivers.

"Damn, my arm's going to fall off before these ponies stop," I heard one of the other driver say.

"Don't worry, we're about to have a winner," said Astor.

"Correct my Lord, Debra just collapsed and she's not moving," said the bastard who had plans to buttfuck me.

"Come on Sofia keep moving! You can still keep up without that skank's help," I heard someone in the crowd shot.

"I believe she is done for as well," I heard Lord Astor say. Then there was the even more ominous "One! Two! Three! Four!"

The counting continued, being taken up by the crowd as well. It seemed forever until I heard the sweetest number ever; ten!

Once I heard Lord Astor shout that number; I stopped.

Panting for breath, too sore and too horny to care that I had won, I just stood there waiting to be released.

"Well my friends the losers service the crowd and the winners the drivers. Lord Astor as befits your position, which one do you wish to fuck first. The redhead or the brunette?" I heard one of the drivers ask.

Oh hells no! I might be horny but I was not going to be kept in this position to be the fuckbitch for men who had just stopped whipping the hell out of me! We'd won; this pony had had it. I kicked off the pony trainers.

"Wait what she doing?" asked someone.

They'd know soon enough.

Planting my feet I change the direction of my force. Instead of pushing forward I lifted up with the full strength of my shoulders and legs. The wooden rail while thick was well aged and very dry. It couldn't take the strain and with a loud crack it broke. Suddenly I was standing at my full height, the broken rail across my shoulder with a very surprised Susa next to me swinging with an inch between her toes and the ground.

The crowd was silent.

But I wasn't done. The links that held the cuffs to the rails while shinny were really poor quality steel. I started to pull down hard and soon one link and then the other broke freeing my hands.

I next ripped the bridle off my head and looked around at the drivers and stage managers. All seemed cowed by the strength I'd displayed. They were used to slaves, and submissives in these contests. Those who'd played by the rules, or didn't have a choice to but follow them.

I was neither.

I stared up at the crowd bloody, bruised but also defiant and victorious.

"My friend and I have won this contest. It's over. Now!" I shouted.

"Anyone disagree?" I asked a dangerous lilt to my

voice.

I think at least one of the Compact fops pissed himself.

"Right then, if you'll excuse me I'd like to get back to what I was doing before all this started," I said as I turned towards Susa.

The warlock had somehow gotten out her cuffs as well, stood there waiting with a lustful looked in her eye. Seeing that she now had my attention she moved forward and with a hard embrace kissed me.

"Let's get out of here and back to our room. I don't know about you but I'm about ready to explode," she whispered to me after she removed her lips from mine.

"One last thing," I told her.

I removed my tail and turning to the drivers asked, "Which one of you thought that I'd be well gaped but still tight enough for a hard fuck?" I asked.

No one said anything but they all looked at one driver in particular.

I smiled my friendliest smile at him as I moved towards him. He bought it because he smiled back.

"Let's see how you like to be gaped," I said as I folded him over my fist with one hard punch.

In a perfect position to allow it to occur, I pulled down his tights and gave him a new appendage.

Maybe the gods had heard prayers after all. The driver was also a redhead.

"Now where were we? Oh yes," I said to Susa as I swept her over my shoulder yet again and headed back to our room.

As we left, I heard the crowd start to chant.

"Blood Princess, Blood Princess, Blood Princess,"

# Chapter 5

"Annie, Annie you there girl?" asked Susa as she snapped her fingers in front of my face.

I shook my head; I was back in hot bath, with Susa.

"Oookayy. That's interesting," I said my head swimming I was still try to reconcile what was going on.

"You were gone for a few seconds. Just staring into astral space, where did you go?"

I quickly brought Susa up to speed as to what I had just experienced. She didn't say anything as I described the contest between us vs. Debra and Sofia.

Only once I was done did she saying anything. "Flashback. You just suffered a flashback, you remembered the events last night as if you'd experienced them for the first time, complete with the same emotional intensity. I've heard of this as a side effect with Fey Brandy Wine and some other causes but it's the first time I've ever seen the effect,"

"So all of it did happen?" I asked.

"Right down to the chanting as you carried me once again off the stage," replied Susa with a smile.

"By the way, you were magnificent. I've been in combat with others, and I've seen you in a fight. But I've never seen anyone pull off the stunts you did last night. I through it was over when you stumbled. But then you got up and started to move even faster than before. I was running just to keep up with the pace you were setting, let alone actually helping to turn that bloody stone."

"Yeah that was strange, I was so aroused at that point that all I felt were those damned feathers. Everything else just became a secondary distraction. At worst it added to what I was already feeling."

"You entered slave space," said Susa.

"Slave space?" I asked. Being naked in a hot tub was the last place I expected to have my vocabulary expanded.

"This is sorta hard to explain. I know from personal experience that people can endure more pain while fucking than the normally could. Part of most sex slave training is to build on that. They allow their bodies to become over stimulated so that their minds can no longer register pleasure or pain. Just the fact they're being stimulated. It's like a warm ocean of feelings, and in it I was able to survive the session, please my mistress, and still sane afterwards."

I nodded, sort of understanding what Susa was saying. I also noticed but did not mention how she went from 'they' too 'I' in the description. Was that how she survived her training? But I had a more important question for her.

"But I was still me during all that, and what about the breaking of the shaft after?"

Susa let out a deep sign buying herself time before she answered.

"You're a masochist, Annie, to put it bluntly you get sexually aroused by pain and to some degree, it's not a bad thing," Susa said quickly, the sick feeling in my stomach must have translated onto my face.

"It doesn't mean you're bent or cursed or a scion of the King Below, it's just an aspect of the chaotic mass we call life," she continued.

"Are you sure?" I asked. I suddenly felt very cold despite being in a near boiling bath, and curled up into ball.

Seeing my pain, Susa did for her an unexpected thing. She came over hugged me and gave me a gentle kiss on the cheek. She then took my one of hands into hers and said. "Of course I'm sure. I'm the mistress of all things perverse and sexual, and this barely rates,"

"It also has some advantages. Think about the pace you set after you stumbled. Not to mention breaking the beam and ending the contest. I've seen you in a fight and I've seen others like you in a fight. There is no way in the Nine Hells that you could have done that without being in the head space you were."

I thought about it for a second. What Susa said made sense and looking back at it I'd never been able to push myself as hard as I did during that contest. And breaking that beam? That was something new. I realized that Susa was right. There was a power there one that I felt a strong desire to explore. I just didn't know how. Though one last detail still bothered me.

"What if all this is true but it only comes out when I'm under the effects of Fey Brandy Wine?" I asked, giving voice to my concern.

Instead of answering directly Susa just took the back of my hand and brought it to her lips. After kissing it she turned it in her hand and started kissing my palm then worked down the inside of my arm. By the time she had reached my elbow with her lips, her other hand was between my legs fingering my clit ring. I was no longer cold.

"Why don't we test that idea and find out?" she asked.

Sounded like a good plan to me.

# Chapter 6

So that's the story. That's how I became the Blood Princess. Actually I usually end the story with me carrying Susa out of the theatre. Of course there are still parts of the tale but only four people (now five including Ricci after the little bitch wormed the story out of me) know the rest.

Like how the fucking that Susa and I did pretty much set the pattern for anytime we hooked up. It was intense, long and rough. At the end of it we both had a fresh batch of scratches and bruises, not to mentions bite marks. Another long bath was required ease the pain all over again.

It was during the second bath that the outside world finally decided to let itself be known. We heard a knock on the door and the Dwarf who had transformed me into the Blood Princess came in followed by several attendants all bearing suites of leather armour.

It turned out he had been inspired and had worked all night on our designs.

This is how the armour that I and my Black Bitches wear came to be designed by a Brothels' fetish designer.

It was during the fitting that Susa and I found out the impact we had during the night. Turns out that the Dark Queen had a 'record night to surpass all record nights'. As our Dwarf designer put it, there wasn't an unstretched hole or virgin hogshead in the place. The Dark Queen had made so much money that we weren't being charged for the room or the damages to the theatre. I later found out that certain slaves and former slaves were also very happy about Debra being banished and they'd let that be known to sympatric ears within the Brothels' owners.

After the fitting, it was evening again. Susa and I had made great plans to go out once again. But given what we'd had endured over the past 48 hours the closest we made it to the outside getting that damned chain off our ankles.

It was early morning the next day when Lia and Gwen finally tracked us down. Gwen was about ready to invoke the Lightbearer's wrath on the door before Lia simple picked the lock. I'm not sure what they were expecting, but I think it wasn't my new look or Susa and I waking up after a night of 'just sleeping' in bed.

Luckily my two sisters forgave us once they tried out the bath. Not to mention the 'no bed head' hair magic we arranged for both of them to get.

They didn't find the story about the Blood Princess and her Black Bitches that amusing however. Gwen in particular was a bit upset since she had come up with idea of us being an adventuring group in the first place.

They'd changed their tune pretty quick though when the job offers had come in.

This is again something I never bring up. The Blood Princess had given a memorable performance at the Dark Queen. So the sex slaves and paid whores started to quietly mention that the Blood Princess headed an adventuring company to their bed mates. Yup the success of the Black Bitches is because a bunch of horny Compactors have tied my name to a sado-masochistic sex contest, and they thought that if they hired me they'd get lucky.

By now I sure you've counted and are wondering who the fourth person is who knows the full story. Well that would be Brutal.

After things had settled down a bit, I went to talk with Gwen about how everything including Susa's assertion that I was a masochist.

I'm a bit ashamed to say that I underestimated my sister both as family and as a cleric of the Sun God.

She listened calmly, smiled at times when I really needed that positive emotion, and in the end gave me a hug and complimented me on the courage it took for me to talk to her.

"Too many people try to hide these aspects of themselves. This is why it so often gets expressed negatively. At some point they've met a follower of the One Eyed God of Secrets, or the King Below, and they've been told that their feelings or desires are shameful. That's what people like Debra like to exploit."

"Oh and the Lightbearer is different?" I challenged.

"He commands us to bring light to the dark places. That just isn't physically but spiritually as well. We help people discover their whole selves. Once we do that, we try and help them find ways to become comfortable with that whole.

"By the way I agree with Susa, this is aspect of yourself you need to explore and become comfortable with. It has a power. One that had already saved Susa from a bet she should not have made," said Gwen.

"So how do I do that?" I asked.

"Come with me. I there is someone I'd like to introduce to you," said Gwen.

After a short cab ride we ended up in front of a small warehouse in one of the more respected sections of the city.

We entered a through a side door and I was stunned by what I saw.

Inside the warehouse was the most well equipped dungeon that I have ever seen. Cages, rakes, chains hooks, and other instruments of pain and torture filled the space.

"A dungeon? You brought me to a torture pit?" I asked Gwen

Moving towards one set of manacles she brought the wrist cuff up for me to examine closer.

"Take a closer look," she said.

I did so and realized two things. First, the chain and cuff were immaculately clean. Second, the cuff was padded.

I looked over to Gwen confused.

"Reverend Gwen! To what do I owe the pleasure?" I heard a deep voice behind me.

Turning I was greeted with the site of one of the largest Half-Orcs I'd ever met. Close to 7 feet tall this Half-Orc looked like he could handle himself in a fight.

"Brutal!" said Gwen moving past me and embracing the Half-Orc.

"Brutal, this is my sister Annie. Annie this is Brutal,

one of the Gates' best dominants."

"Like Debra?" I asked.

Brutal snorted in disgust. I could tell I just hit a sore spot.

"No Brutal doesn't top slaves. He tops free people like you; masochists, submissives, switches and others who just aren't sure what they are," said Gwen quickly correcting my mistake.

"I have rules, and my relationships are built on trust and mutual respect. Not fear and humiliation," said Brutal.

"Annie, several members of my church work with Brutal to explore what their particular fetish means to them in a larger context," said Gwen.

"And some should instead of seeking other more destructive means," said Brutal looking pointedly at Gwen.

"Annie, you were looking for a safe place to explore what happened to you. This is the best place to do that," said Gwen.

I paused. The Dark Queen had opened a door that I did not, could not, close again. Once more I thought of the millstone and moving forward one step at a time never stopping.

Time to take another step.

"Where do we start?" I asked Brutal.

**Leveling: The Blood Princess Saga
Bonus Story**


Takes place between A Night at the Dark
Queen and Ice and Pride

# Acknowledgements

This bonus short story for Beyond the Gates is directly the result of one of my test readers Shawn L. He really liked the character Ricci and throughout reading Ice and Pride he kept asking if I'd write something from Ricci's perspective. When I thought about putting together a collection of the first three Blood Princess novellas I decided to add a bonus short story; and thanks to Shawn, Ricci was at the fore front of my thoughts.

So Shawn this is all you fault.

"Well if this doesn't instill a sense of shared suffering, and encourage working as a team, I'm not sure what will," said Susa as she walked around both Annie and me.

Once again the black haired, and if you ask me black hearted, woman had talked my Mistress into a masochist exercise cloaked as a contest. When it came to sex, the warlock could be extremely adept at turning my Mistress's perceived strengths into weaknesses. In this case she got my red haired Mistress to agree by framing the scene as a new way to allow her to test and push past her limits. I got voluntold (does this term even exist in the Gates?) to participate in the contest by Mistress acting, again under Susa's 'influence', like the owner of the submissive sex slave I had agreed to be when we first met.

As I said Susa is a manipulative bitch, but I'll give her, her due, when it comes to scenes she's a creative domme. Take the one Mistress and I were currently involved in for instance. It started with two solid metal poles about two feet high spaced about a foot apart. The top of the poles were enchanted so that it could take on a variety of shapes. For this scene, they were in the shape of a woman's hand. Susa then had Mistress and I face each other; our pussies each right above one of the poles. Mistress and I knew what ultimately we were going to end up doing, but Susa, in her sadistic best, delayed things as long as possible.

First she bounded our hands high between our shoulder blades. This forced our breasts forward for maximum exposure, it also left our lower backs and asses uncovered for any 'motivations', that Susa wanted to employ. Next Susa fingered both of us, to near climax. She's very skilled at this and despite my reluctance in being a part of this 'contest' her kneading, pinching, and caressing soon had me hot and my pussy wet. Seeing Mistress becoming aroused as well, I surrendered to the inevitable leaned forward and kissed her hard on the lips. A wave of genuine pleasure washed over me as I tasted my Mistresses lips and she let out a groan of pleasure and need that had nothing to do with what the bitch was doing between our legs.

Once Susa had gotten us to the right temperature, she strapped on a pair of six inch slave trainers on to our feet. These metal spiked sandals forced the wearer to stay high on the balls of their feet. The alternative was to drive the metal spike deep up into your heel.

Susa's final piece of prep work was to connect our nipples together with circular needles. As the sharpened end ran through the top of Mistress's right nipple and out the bottom she took it with all the stoicism (again is that even a word here?) you would expect from a fighting woman, letting out only a short hiss of pain. I on the other hand, in comparison am a wimp. My breathing increased and I let out a cry of pain that got disapproving glances from both women. The layer of sweat that was a constant with living in the City of Gates caused the welling blood to run from both holes in my nipple, down my breast, and on over my stomach.

I find it interesting that Susa and Mistress first encountered these particular restraining devices when they were tortured by house Hector almost a year ago. That someone who's supposedly a 'responsible' domme would use such devices was a surprise to me. However, in a world where blemish free magical healing is cheap and easily available, the breadth of what is considered 'responsible' is greatly expanded.

When the warlock threaded the second needle through my left tit, Susa had to grab onto my breast to keep it steady enough. At least that time I managed to keep from crying out; but only by biting my lower lip till it bled. Once the needles were through all four nipples, Susa said a command word that caused their ends to connect, bringing our tits into tantalising contact.

"Well done Ricci," Mistress whispered to me when Susa left us alone for a few seconds. When Susa returned she was ready to begin.

"Alright ladies you know what happens next. Try and work together or you might end up ripping your tits off," she said as I felt her braided leather switch burn an angry red welt on my ass. This was followed by a similar lash across Mistress's butt.

Both of us started to squat down over our individual metal hand. Despite the Gate's night being its usual hot and humid self, the hands were surprisingly cold and both of us gasped as our bodies touch the metal limbs. However, Mistress didn't allow the temperature of the metal to slow her pace; and if I wanted to keep my breasts intact I'd have to keep up. On our first squat we only got thumb deep, before rising. It was Mistress who set the pace to one that I could follow; part of the unspoken teamwork that we were going to need to survive this contest.

Another of the modifications that had been done to me was that I'm permanently virgin tight. A pixie could fuck me and he'd complain about how hard it was to get his dick in me. Mistress knew this, so she took in less than she could before she started to rise. Once we got to the top knuckle of the metal hand's ring finger Mistress started to squat down again, this time taking in a little more of the hand before rising.

Unfortunately, Susa wanted a faster pace and used the switch to transmit this desire. We increased our speed and with a lot of grunting and groaning on both our parts, we heated and lubed the hands to where we could take the complete metal limb into ourselves.

After a few more squats though, the drive of the contest and the eagerness for an orgasm caused Mistress to set a more vigorous pace, which Susa encouraged us to keep. We continued the squat fuck for several minutes as the pain of an unfulfilled climax grew to dominate our thinking. But the toll our exertions were taking on the other parts of our bodies were starting to tell. My calves were burning and despite our rhythm both Mistress's and my tits were bleeding as our forced nipple, play stretched them back and forth. Mistress being a true masochist channeled all this discomfort into desire. Looking into her glassy eyes and swollen lips I could tell she was about to pop. While I was relieved that this damned contest was going to end soon, a tiny part of me was sorry that it was Mistress and not I about to cum.

Which was why the scream of pain followed by Mistress's standing so quickly that it almost torn the rings out of my nipples came as such a surprise.

"The fuck? Susa!" she cried at the little warlock.

"Oh didn't I tell you? The scene ends when you climax together. If either of you is about to cum without the other, you get shocked," Susa said so innocently that I almost believed that she had 'forgotten' to tell us. Then with a solid swack from her switch, she added, "Now back to it."

Mistress could have said Susa's safe word at that moment and ended the scene. But, she prided herself in always finishing what she started. Susa knew this and I got the sick feeling she wanted to see how far Mistress was willing to push things when others were involved. As a domme, Susa liked testing the whole person with her scenes, not just physically but mentally, morally as well.

Apparently we'd not reached that point yet, because I saw that determined look in Mistress's eyes and sneer on her face. The Blood Princess had come out to play. Going down again she was back to taking the full hand within three squats, and the rhythm of our fisting increased from the already frantic pace we'd previously set. While my desire built once again to painful levels, the burning fatigue in my legs also increased and threatened to overwhelm me. I so wanted to slow down; to stop but Susa's switch kept our pace steady. Moreover, despite the even tempo of our squats, our heavier breathing made it impossible for us not to pull and twist our nipples in painful contortions.

The scene became a blur as I finally hit my pain threshold and endorphins flooded my system. My mind floated in and out of reality and it decided at this time to remind me that when a body feels physically done and it can go no further a person has reached only forty percent of what it was actually capable of doing. From which world I got that fact from I'm not sure. I think it was from the old one because that world seemed obsessed with numbers.

As that factoid worked around my head, I felt the Blood Princess's tongue move past my lips as she Frenched me.

"Come on Ricci don't give in on me now. Susa will never let us live this one down if we give in," she said when she pulled back from the kiss.

"She's right about that," said Susa matter-of-factly as she brought that damned switch down across our breasts.

"Concentrate on our tits," I know you like it when we nipple play. Just concentrate on that and only that," the Blood Princess said to me.

I did as the Blood Princess said and concentrated as best I could on the feeling of our nipples playing with each other and it did help. Despite the burning calves, the welts across my ass and lower back and my bleeding tits my arousal once again grew.

"I'm going to cum," I heard myself say.

"So am I," groaned the Blood Princess. "On three!"

"One, two, threeee," we said together, the orgasm hit, and the real world went away for a bit.

***

When the room came back into focus, Mistress and I were off the metal hands and we were lying on our sides still panting. Susa, was taking off the slave trainers and rubbing our legs to help with the burn.

"Well done both of you," she said. "I wasn't sure if you'd make it. That scene needed both teamwork and leadership. Annie you pushed both to a new level. In addition, Ricci broke through a new endurance level. Well done both of you."

Mistress and I only mumbled our thanks. I was exhausted and hurt pretty much everywhere. But, I was there enough to do a mental double take when Susa asked Mistress "So did you find out what you wanted?

"Yes, and you're right I'd never would have gone far enough to really push her to her limit," replied Mistress.

"See I told you it's a lot harder to be a dominant than it looks. Remember that next time you spend the evening with Brutal and remember nothing says thank you to a man like blowing him without being asked to," said Susa

I must have had a confused look on my face, because without even being prompted Susa said "It was a leveling exercise. Annie wanted to be a better domme for you, but had problems with how far to take things. Both Brutal and I tried to explain it to her, but you know words and Annie don't play well together."

"Hey!" Annie interrupted.

Susa ignored Mistress and continued. "Brutal and I thought that a leveling scene would get Annie to where she needed to be. She was actually the domme in charge but she was experiencing everything with you so that she could physically get an idea of where your limits were, how to recognize the signs and just how far you could push things. I was here just to monitor and keep things running at your pace."

As Susa talked I turned and looked at my Mistress "you went through all that just to try and be a better owner?" I asked my heart in my throat.

"Yes, of course you're worth it?" she replied.

I didn't say another word but instead threw my arms around Mistress's neck and kissed her soundly.

"Well my work here appears done, so I'll just leave you two lovers," Susa said getting up to leave.

Susa's assumption was wrong. Mistress grabbed up the rope that had bound her hands and tackled Susa, pinning the smaller woman beneath her. The warlock was a nasty close in fighter but she was no match for Mistress, and soon Susa was on her stomach her wrists tied to her ankles in a leg spreading hogtie exposing her sex.

Susa looked up at Mistress with a surprised look clearly on her face.

"As you say Susa, I should say a proper thank you to my domes. I know you're a switch and you don't often get a chance to be the bottom. Besides 'Oh did I forget to tell you?' My tight fucking ass; you're going to pay for that one Susa," said Mistress to the little warlock.

Turning to me she said. "Ricci did you clean and put away that discipline strap-on that Susa had you use on me last week?"

"The one with the three dildos? Yes Mistress I know exactly where it is," I said catching onto what Mistress had in mind. "And might I suggest the knotted Gnoll dick polymorph?"

Mistress just smiled and said, "I'll leave that to you since you're the one who's going to wear it. I'm going to have my pussy licked for the next hour or so,"

"Of course Mistress, your command is my wish." I said gleefully wanting to also say 'Thank you'.

***

When I finally awoke from our night of sexual debauchery (or Tuesday, as I know it) we were well into the heat of the afternoon. Mistress lived near the Dark Queen in a penthouse of an eight-floor walk-up (all this damn magic and no one has come up with a magic elevator). As usual I was the last awake. Susa was sitting in the direct sunlight without even sweating her nose buried in a book that was half her size. Which meant the grunting that I heard from the next room was Mistress doing her morning exercise routine and not another bout of sex.

"Morning, sleep well?" asked Susa sweetly like the sadist she truly was.

I grunted a warning at the warlock about not being too cheerful and stumbled to the bathroom. Unlike everyone else, I've met on this world I am not a morning person. I lurched over to the toilet and with an ungraceful thump sat down. One of the reasons why my Mistress paid extra for the penthouse was the built in bathroom. As I got rid of unwanted weight, I once again marveled on how similar the remembered parts of my old life are to this new life. My old self remembered her history lessons in school, and at movies, about medieval societies, which the City of Gates at first resembles. How dirty they were with shit being thrown out onto the streets, bathing being seen as a sin; and how diseases killed millions because they didn't understand basic sanitation or how illness spread.

But then I also don't recall magic being a part of medieval societies, nor a God who was actually willing to explain what bacteria were. Let alone clerics and lay persons having magical rituals to cure disease. My new life however, has such Gods: As a result, the mortal sections of the city, and the people living there, are amazingly clean and disease free; early childhood mortality is also low and people are healthy considering they're living in the middle of a jungle.

Once I'd finished my morning routine, which included a quick shower, I flipped my hair to activate the magic to get it back into the salon fresh style I've had since I arrived. What other women pay a dozen pieces of gold for was 'standard equipment' for a high end pleasure slave like me. Once more presentable, and feeling as much like a human being as I can without my morning coffee I re-entered the living room to see if Mistress needs anything.

She'd finished her morning exercise and was now oiling and sharpening her vast number of knives and daggers. As usual when she was at home, Mistress was completely naked; the welts and bruises of last night's contest clearly visible. However, they did little to detract from her beauty. Granted she has had some work done, nowhere near what Susa and I were subjected too, but her breasts wouldn't have past the pencil test. The tight muscular body though was all natural. She moved with a predatory grace that attracted a lot of attention even in a city renowned for female beauty. I recall the first time we fucked and how wonderful it felt to have the powerful form rubbing next to mine, drinking in her musk, her taste and the thrill of being so dominated by such a powerful; creature.

But this morning I was greeted by a sunny smile and genuine pleasure.

"Morning sleepy head I see you're finally awake," she said.

"Good morning Mistress is there anything that you need?" I ask.

She picked up the empty tankard near her and passed it to me, "Another fifty/fifty and I imagine that Susa will want more coffee. Oh and get out some fruit and cheese," she replied without even thinking about it. When I first started living with Mistress, she had tried very hard not to treat me like a servant but more like a prolonged houseguest. However, as the weeks past, she realized that I was more than willing to do all the unpleasant chores around the apartment. Mistress started to treat me more and more like a servant. I still paid rent and half the food bill (even though I ate maybe a third of the food we buy). I don't mind being treated this way; it was part of the gig I signed up for, when I convinced Mistress to keep me as a slave.

Heading to the kitchen I got out a mug and poured what remained of the first pot of coffee into it. The coffee was still hot, and thanks to Susa's tastes very strong. Without even thinking about it I down half the mug, sighing contently as the caffeine hit my system. I also counted two of my many blessings: That like Susa I'm immune to the effects of normal fires and heat; like scalding hot coffee and that this world had the equivalent to Columbian Dark Roast.

Now willing to face a world that included more than just my Mistress I went out to collect Susa's mug, confirmed that she indeed wanted more coffee and if cheese and fruit will be sufficient for breakfast.

"Yes to both," she said without even looking up from her book. Like Mistress and I the warlock hadn't bothered with clothing. Her black and white appearance with the long red welts parallel to her spine from Mistress's 'encouragement' reminded me of that old joke about newspapers. Turning I suddenly felt her cold hand on my ass, her thumb running across one of the many welts she put there.

"I hope I didn't hurt you too badly last night, I had to push things or Annie wouldn't have gotten the idea of how far she could go with you," she said in a feeble apology.

I shrugged "the circle needles were a bit much," I said looking down at my still tender nipples.

"Ahhh but they make forced nipple play so much

easier and admit it you like rubbing against Annie's tits for that long," she said her voice growing more husky as she talked.

Without waiting for an answer her hand moved down my ass to between my legs. "You got wet just thinking about her tits didn't you? You little slut," she stated the fact.

"I think I deserve a reward for figuring out a way of connecting you two for so long. Don't you?" Susa asked as she spread her legs exposing the black, swollen lips of her pussy to me.

That I was horny by just thinking about Mistress I found frustrating, but I also thought that Susa had a point. She did deserve a gift for what she did with us last night; and it really wouldn't take that long to get her off.

"Gwen would skin both of us alive if she knew you were using magic on Ricci to get her to go down on you; you do remember that," I heard Mistress warn Susa from the dining room. "And she'd do it with her tongue and an evil glare.

Susa then sighed and closed her legs, and suddenly I was wondering why I had thought it was a good idea. "Bitch," I mouthed at her.

"Can't blame a girl for trying, and you're really good with your tongue," was her reply.

I gave her the finger, (a gesture that was unknown in this world till I introduced it) and headed back to the kitchen.

Once there I reloaded the coffee machine pronounce the command word to get it working, and got out the cheese and fruit from the cooler. I then sighed and returned to the living room and collected *all* the kitchen knives that Mistress had once again sharpened to an inch of their lives and return to the kitchen thinking that if she started to sharpen the spoons I *would* demand my freedom.

"Pardon?" asked Mistress.

I redden; not realizing that I had said something allowed, "I said that you have enough time to wash before breakfast Mistress," I responded quickly keeping my back to her so that she couldn't see my face.

Returning to the kitchen I put two of the kitchen knives back into their holders and kept out the third to cut the cheese and fruit into something that at least looked like civilized portions. By that time the coffee was done and I refilled both Susa's and mine mug. Taking the high road I didn't spit into Susa's coffee. I then got out what passes for fresh blood orange juice (Mistress got hooked on the stuff as soon as she heard the name. She really does take things too far in my opinion) and filled the tankard half way and added water for fill it.

I returned to the dining room and gently moved Mistress's knives off half the table and set it for our first meal of the day.

"Come and get it," I said in a louder than normal voice to get people's attention. I placed half the meal in front of Mistress and divvied up the remainder between myself and Susa.

The brunette came in and goosed me before she sat down. Mistress, who was just toweling off from her shower, sat down leaving the wet towel on the floor for me to pick up. She barely got out a thank you before she tore into her food with the same gusto that she did most things.

Susa ate with just a little less enthusiasm and both were finished long before I was done. Mistress sat back and enjoyed a few minutes of just doing nothing, while Susa drank her coffee. I saw the wheels in her head turning glancing between me and Mistress, and I wondered what she was up to *this* time.

"So what were your plans for the day?" Susa asked. The Black Bitches were between jobs so for everyone but me their time was their own.

"Ulric should be done with my armour today so I was

planning on going to the Dark Queen and picking it up. Then; I don't know maybe hit the gym and spar a bit. Why do you have a better idea?"

"A new group of players have arrived from the outer Chaos. They supposedly have an original work that combines ice and lightening that shouldn't be missed," said Susa.

"I don't know, modern theatre and dance really don't interest me," replied Mistress.

"You *can not* compare what I've talking about to the morality plays that Gwen forces us to go to. This is far more like being on Fey Brandywine; only this time no hangover or blackouts," replied Susa.

"But it still includes getting naked and being turned into a pony?" asked Mistress.

"You really don't like exploring new things do you?" said Susa.

"No I'm fine exploring new things, only when I do it with you the track record is me ending up naked, tied up and fucked," replied Mistress.

"You make that sound like a bad thing," said Susa with a smile.

Mistress just gave Susa a withering look.

"Okay how about this, come with me to see the performance and if your mind isn't blown I'll come with you to Brutal's dungeon for the next month," said Susa.

*That* got my attention; Brutal was Mistress's dom and a very competent one at that. He was also one of the few people who wasn't impressed with, or afraid of Susa. After what I endured last night, I would pay to see what he'd come up with as a scene for them both to share.

I could tell the idea interested Mistress, but she wasn't sure.

"Go ahead Mistress; I'll pick up your armour. You take your time to get ready for the show and go out and have a good time tonight.

Both of the girls looked at me like neither had been expecting me to speak let alone actually give my opinion.

I gave them my best smile and then took a long sip of my coffee.

"See even Ricci thinks you should try new things," said Susa using my agreement to press her position.

"Alright, alright I'll go," Mistress finally relented.

"Excellent!" said Susa who then turned to me and said "Ricci why don't you head out and collect Annie's armour after you finish your breakfast?"

"Because it's the heat of the day and we're in a heat wave. Not even an Englishman is crazy enough to go out in this heat," I replied to Susa's question.

Too late did I realize that I'd once again said something that made sense in my old life, not the new one. I'd killed the conversation as both of the girls looked me with blank 'what the fuck?' looks on their faces.

I drained my coffee "why don't I just head down to the Dark Queen and get Mistress's armour?" I then said, while I polished off the last bit of cheese and orange on my plate.

"Sounds like a plan," said Mistress.

\*\*\*

One of the things I've been asked by people who know my story, is do I remember enough of my old life to miss it? The answer complicated because while I can't remember actual memories when I try and remember my old life, strong emotions do rise to the surface. Mostly these emotions revolve around safety, the near narcotic feeling of blissful joy (usually centred on vague memories of shopping), and a desperate fear of being bored. What feelings of excitement and thrills I appear to be related to things that had the illusion of danger. Words like rollercoasters and suspense movies come to mind but to be honest I have no image to put to those words. I know some of my tattoos like the bird on my right breast date from that time, and I *think* I was sexually submissive, and walked on the sexual wild side in the old world (which puts me square in the normal space in the Gates).

So to summaries; the emotions I recall from the old world are safe, bliss, and boredom; broken by the occasional false thrill from a movie or finding a really nice pair of shoes on seveny percent off.

In the Gates, the chief emotions were watchfulness, excitement, a healthy dose of paranoia *and* awe. When I first walked the streets of the Gates with Mistress I blurted out "Its New York on acid!" While I couldn't explain what I meant I still stand behind those words; they just seemed right.

It was the press of mortals of literally all shapes, sizes and colours; that caused that impact upon me I believe. I have a strong suspicion that my old life's world only had Human's, inhabiting it. I had heard of Dwarves, Elves, Goblins, and such but I nearly creamed myself when I met real Elves like Lia and Gwen. It took me weeks to truly feel they were real and I wasn't fantasising; and the less said about how embarrassed I made Mistress feel when I totally geeked out seeing my first Giant the better. And we wont even mention the D creatures, Dragons, Devils, Demons, and Drow, sorry *Dark Elves*. Every time I'm out on the streets I have to be careful not to gawk at some new creature I've just encountered.

It's not because of embarrassment that I'm afraid of gawking, it because if I'm gawking I've left myself vulnerable for a moment in the City of Gates; and such vulnerabilities are extremely dangerous. The city is full of predators, not just your usual pickpockets, muggers, and confidence men, but slavers, ghouls, minor demons or worst; looking for a quick snack. While the city isn't so dangerous that as soon as you're distracted they descend it's best not to make a habit of it; especially if you're a slave. In the City of Gates slaves *are* property so if someone decides to have some fun at my expense it's the equivalent of vandalism. So while on the streets the safest thing to do is stay in crowds, keep aware of your surroundings and walk like your owner is half a step behind you.

Unfortunately during the heat of the day all three of those are hard to pull off. First there are no crowds, in fact afternoon is the quietest time in the city day or night. Second the humidity is so oppressive that it's hard not to keep your head down and concentrate on just moving forward. Finally with so few people around it's clear if you're alone. Still I didn't stand out too much despite being completely naked.

In a place as hot and humid as the Gates the vast majority of working people walk around in only a loin cloth. According to Mistress most children, no matter what their background, don't wear clothing at all for the first decade of their lives. The only way to tell the rich from the poor kids is the value of the body jewelry. Maybe that's the reason why body modification is so popular in the Gates. With all that skin you need to use tattoos, piercings and thanks to the abundance of magic, body augmentation just to standout. My old life had a lot of plastic people in it but I do not believe that at least the humans of the Gates, had *that* many naturally perky 34Cs, or the average male's junk was ten inches long.

Knowing that, I kept running from one small crowd in the shade to the next, as I headed towards the Dark Queen with the confidence of knowing that I was never the most remodeled person on the street.

"Hey guys look at the silver haired one! Looks like she was a bad girl last night," someone shouted from the shadows of the narrow allyway across the street.

Fuck: Well never the most modified *accept* for the fact

that my lower back, ass, and thighs were crisscrossed with fresh welts.

I kept walking, hoping that the voice and his friends were just interested in looking and calling out 'bad girls'. However I was soon surrounded by half a dozen mortals who were in their late teens to early twenties. All were scruffy looking as if they'd miss a bath, shave and hair cut, along with several meals recently. All wore loin cloths with a couple too brief to hold in their obviously growing erections. The lot were also armed with a collection of long daggers, knives and short swords or clubs. They all looked like they were familiar with violence though none of them looked truly dangerous. In other words typical street toughs and bullies who thought they owned a block.

"Where you going?" one asked.

"Has someone been a bad girl?" asked another.

"Let me kiss it and make it feel better," said a third.

Outside the circle of toughs the other city dwellers looked away. None of them wanted to get cross the group that runs this street for just a slave girl that no local owns.

I glanced up at them showing that I wasn't afraid, but not to challenge any of them. "Guys I'd love to chat really, I'm on an errand for my Mistress the Blood Princess and she's expecting me back soon." Mistress is well enough known among the professional thief guilds that dropping her name might have gotten these guys to back off.

"Who in the Nine Hells is the Blood Princess," asked the one who wanted to kiss me all better.

Well so much for Plan A, now it was either let these guys have me and hope they were only interested in a quick fuck or Plan B. Given the hungry look in their eyes I decided on Plan B; no witnesses.

I stepped towards the tough who was closest to the dark alleyway; I gave him a wink and said with as much honesty as I could muster "you really shouldn't follow me,"

I then kneed him in the crotch. He was fast enough that

I hit more thigh than balls, but it was enough to open a hole in the flesh ring around me to slip through. Escape now possible I bolted through the hole and the chase is on.

The audacity of my attack surprised the group enough that I got a few precious seconds of running time before they started after me. The twit that I kicked also groaned loud enough to attract the attention of more people and I heard a ripple of laughter as I entered the alley. I ran as fast as my modified legs allowed me to, but I knew these guys were faster. Fortunately the alley quickly intersected with a larger one that ran between the housing block's rear entrances. The alley was covered with garbage, both solid and not so solid, and I was able to run over and between the piles keeping them between me and my pursuers. At first I heard a lot of cursing behind me but Mistresses workouts often include running. I might not be able to beat these guys in a sprint but a marathon? Soon the toughs stop wasting breath swearing and they just keep running trying to catch up.

Between breaths I curse their idiocy. This chase is now as much about losing face as it is about lust. No way can the street toughs let me escape now. That would be too high a loss of street cred and the potential of others seeing them as weak.

Finally I spot the kind of exit from the alleyway that I was looking for. Breaking right, I wriggled through a broken gate into an abandoned building. The first floor has a nest of Kobold squatters but I ignore them as I looked for the stairway. Finding it I begin to run up the stairs careful to not trip. The building is another walk up so I keep going up until I no longer see any signs of current habitation. Once I reach that level I head towards one of the rooms on the alley side of the building. One apartment's door is off its hinges and that's the one I entered. With no other way for them to escape I turn and wait, a part of me regretting what I must do next.

I don't have to wait long as the first three entered the room. Angry; they call out to their partners where they are.

"You fucking bitch, you think anyone here going to give a flying fuck about what we do to you?" one of them asked through laboured breathing.

"I was about to ask you the same question?" I say smiling as I thrust my hands towards his chest. Soul Taker, my infernal rune sword forms mid thrust and its point easily enters the tough's naked chest through his heart and out his back. As his life blood sizzles on the sword's blade, my coven with the infernal powers kicks in. Soul Taker lives up to its name as it sucks in part of the tough's soul and an even smaller piece of that soul enters my body. I'm hit with the rush of endorphins that removes all the pain I felt from last night's fun and the flat out running I'd just been doing. Glassy eyed I turn hungrily to the next two. The realization that they were really hunting the wrong prey hits them and they begin to run screaming from the room.

I slammed the point of Soul Taker into the floor while I spoke a word of command. Through sheer force of will I directed the magical energies I had summoned through the sword. Gouts of flames erupt from the runes and the two toughs are turned into so much charcoal. Their bodies hadn't even hit the ground before I was past them; hunting down the last three.

As I cleared the apartment's entrance two of the remaining toughs attack me from either side of the door. They had heard the screams and decided they'd wait in ambush short swords ready. I parry one attack with my sword shearing through the blade's poor steel and deep into the tough's arm opening the limb from wrist to elbow.

The other tough's blade clanks against a shield of emerald energy that forms across my back. My patron made sure that even as a naked slave I am not without defences.

With the first attacker disarmed and screaming I turned quickly and brought Soul Taker down onto the second tough's collar bone. The rune sword clove through the bone, smashed into his rib cage; cutting through lung and heart and it didn't stop until it was buried into the tough's spine.

Of course the big bastard had to fall back leaving me with the choice of holding onto the sword and going over with him or letting go and stay standing. I chose the latter because I knew I still had one last tough to deal with.

Looking over towards the stairs I saw him at the same time he saw me. We stared at each other for what felt like several hours with him looking between me and Soul Taker at least a dozen times before he decided to do something.

He decided that he didn't need to follow his friends over the cliff. Dropping his sword he turned and started to run down the stairs. My bolt of eldritch energy that is the signature of all warlocks took his head off before he got three steps down the stairs.

"I'm a fucking devil cursed superhero you idiot! You don't think I could take out a piece of shit like you at range?" I shout at the headless corpse.

I didn't bother trying to pull Soul Taker out of the tough's spine. Instead I just re-summoned it to my hand. Turning I faced the last alive tough. He'd lost enough blood from his arm that he'd fallen to his knees and was looking around at what remained of this friends not really understanding what had happened.

"In your next life try and figure out who the truly dangerous people really are," I said to him as took his head.

So that was Plan B: Find an isolated area and kill the toughs who weren't paying close enough attention to their world. You see while assaulting or killing a slave is just property crime, a slave who has the balls to actually defend herself and gets caught doing so is given to the Demon Pit as a dinner offering.

It's also is *the* reason why I truly never want to return to my old world. I KNOW that there while I might have money and some degree of fame, but in the Gates I wield magic: a kind of power my old self couldn't even dream of having. That combined with the fact that I live more in one day in the Gates than I did in a year in my old life.

That's worth the occasional night of rough sex.

### 

Thank you for reading my eBook's. If you liked my stories, please go back to the retailer who you downloaded this collection from and leave a short review and rating. It's feedback like that that will help me become a better writer.

# About the Author

Jessica Short has always been a storyteller, either in person, as a gamemaster or as a writer of fiction. However, it wasn't she saw other people putting themselves out there on Deviantart did she work up the courage to show one of her stories to a friend. With his encouragement she finished the story and posted what was the story now titled 'Best Laid Plans' on the website.

The rest as they say, is history.

Read Jessica's Smashwords Interview at https://www.smashwords.com/interview/SandyEA

# Other books by this author

Please visit your favourite ebook retailer to discover other books by Jessica Short:

***The Blood Princess Saga***
Best Laid Plans
Knife Play
A Night at the Dark Queen
Ice and Pride
Beyond the Gates (The Blood Princess Books 1-3)
Means and Ends (Fall 2016)

# Connect with Jessica Short

Here are my social media coordinates:

Favorite my Smashwords author page:
https://www.smashwords.com/profile/view/SandyEA
Visit my website: http://jessica42.deviantart.com/

Made in the USA
San Bernardino, CA
02 May 2017